Her Christmas Redemption

Toni Shiloh

ISBN-13: 978-1-335-58540-0

Her Christmas Redemption

For questions and comments about the quality of this book, please contact us at CustomerService@Harlequin.com.

Love Inspired
22 Adelaide St. West, 41st Floor
Toronto, Ontario M5H 4E3, Canada
www.LoveInspired.com

Printed in U.S.A.

"Tell me all about Christmas Wishes."

Michael nodded. "Throughout fall, people nominate others in need by submitting a name via the mystery box."

"Does that mean we'll pick who gets their wish fulfilled?" Vivian asked.

"Exactly."

A thoughtful look crossed Vivian's face. "How do we choose?"

"The church has the finances set aside. Basically, the allotted amount will determine who gets chosen."

Her face fell. "Could we add to the fund?"

She wanted to *donate*? He hadn't seen that coming.

"Michael?"

He blinked, focusing on Vivian. "Sorry. Um, I don't see a reason why we couldn't."

She nodded, glancing at the simple band on her wrist.

Vivian Dupre was a conundrum. Something about her screamed class, but her outward appearance stated she liked simple things. Which was the truth? The surface appearance or the niggling feeling that raised the hairs on the back of his neck that said there was more to her than meets the eye?

Toni Shiloh is a wife, mom and multipublished Christian contemporary romance author. She writes to bring God glory and to learn more about His goodness. A member of the American Christian Fiction Writers (ACFW) and of the Virginia Chapter, Toni loves connecting with readers via social media. You can learn more about her at tonishiloh.com.

Books by Toni Shiloh

Love Inspired

An Unlikely Proposal
An Unlikely Alliance
Her Christmas Redemption

Visit the Author Profile page at LoveInspired.com.

Thanks be unto God for his unspeakable gift.

—*2 Corinthians* 9:15

To the Author and Finisher of my faith.

Acknowledgments

Writing a novel isn't a solitary effort. I had lots of help along the way, especially from the awesome members in my street team. Thanks to Christina Hess Al-Junaid, Michelle Leverette, Nancy McLeroy, Martha Artyomenko and Necee Lomelino for naming characters and businesses in Willow Springs. Also, special shout-out to my youngest son. I'm still laughing about Billie-ie.

I also want to thank my critique partners and great friends. Andrea Boyd, Sarah Monzon and Jaycee Weaver, you ladies are the best. I am so blessed to have your friendship and wisdom along my writing journey.

Many thanks to the team at Harlequin. Thank you, Dina Davis, for all your hard work and dedication to making this story the best. To the cover designers and all the people I know help but haven't been able to meet. Thank you for spreading this story out to the masses.

I'd like to thank my family for putting up with my deadline tunnel vision but also encouraging me when I have doubts. You guys are the best men I know. Love you to the moon and back.

Chapter One

Vivian Dupre stared at the mountain of a man perched on the ladder hanging Christmas lights on the pale yellow gabled farmhouse with a perfect full-length front porch. The shamrock-colored roof had a tan sign dangling from the fascia with the words General Store & Office. She could just imagine what the place would look like when the sun set and the white twinkle lights came on.

She opened her mouth to get his attention, her breath forming a cloud in the cold winter air. Though they had a little under a month until the calendar welcomed the winter solstice, the temperatures in northwestern Arkansas had already dipped. "Excuse me, are you Michael Wood?"

The man looked over his shoulder, grabbing the edge of the ladder to steady himself. His low-cut fade had sponge twists on top and had been evenly shaped, like the beard and mustache covering the lower half of his face. His brown skin didn't hold a single blemish. Her breath caught at his penetrating stare. His eyes seemed to see right through her, making her feel exposed. Could he tell by a single glance where she'd begun her drive this morning?

She gave herself a mental shake. Of course not. She'd showered and changed into regular clothing instead of the black jumpsuit with County Jail written on the back that she'd sported the past six months.

"Yes, ma'am. You Vivian Dupre?" His voice held just a hint of an accent, as if he'd lived outside Arkansas for a number of years and had learned to curb the Southern inflections.

"I am." Nerves—or the cold—had her toes wiggling in her boots and her legs jiggling back and forth.

The man climbed down the ladder. "Welcome to Simplicity Rentals."

He stuck out a hand that swallowed her palm right up. Her arm tingled from his touch. How long had it been since another person had given her any positive physical contact? *One hundred eighty-five days, but who's counting?*

She jerked her hand back and cleared her throat. "Nice to meet you. I'm here for the long-term rental."

"Right. I've got you all set in one of the tiny homes. Just need you to add your occupation to the rental agreement and sign." He hitched a thumb over his shoulder toward the front door.

Vivian tried for a smile, though her heart hammered. Her parole officer had assured her she didn't need to disclose her incarceration in order to rent with Mr. Wood. Still, what if he discovered her past? Or worse, asked outright?

She forced her thoughts to focus on the tiny home. Her mind couldn't wrap around the idea of staying in a home only two hundred square feet in space. Of course, that size was better than the seventy-square-foot cell she used to reside in.

"Sure. I can do that. I'll be working at the Springs Bible Church."

Michael slid his hands into his flannel jacket. "Are you a…pastor?" Wisps of steam hung in the air between them.

Vivian snorted, then clapped a hand over her mouth, trying to prevent derisive laughter from escaping. *No one* in her former life would ever make that mistake.

But this is the new beginning you wanted. Where your past doesn't exist.

She cleared her throat. "Receptionist."

The job couldn't compare to the career she'd had in Little Rock, but she needed a simpler way of life. *Ha! Simplicity Rentals.* Okay, so she was a dork who spent way too much time making commentary in her head.

"Awesome. We'll miss Ms. Ann but she'll be happy to move on."

"Yes. She's the one who interviewed me." It had been weird discussing a church position while using the jail-house phone. The pastor, Liam Johnson, knew about her misdemeanor but had promised no judgment and to keep her past to himself. Only time would tell if that would prove true.

No way Vivian wanted to see the disgust in these people's eyes that had been visible in those of her ex-friends, ex-coworkers and, worst of all, her parents. She'd love to flush her secret down the drain and never revisit it again.

"Speaking of Ms. Ann…" Michael's voice trailed off as a SUV turned into the makeshift lot in front of the General Store.

A portly woman sporting a black bob exited the sports utility vehicle and rushed over. "Michael, Michael, Michael," she said in a Southern accent thick as gravy. "We need to talk." She halted, realizing he wasn't alone.

Vivian waved.

"I didn't mean to interrupt. You must think I'm a terribly rude person." The woman placed pale hands on rosy cheeks.

"Not at all." Vivian swallowed around the ball of nerves gathering in her throat. "I'm Vivian."

The woman gasped. "Are you really? I'm Ms. Ann. Can I give you a hug? I'm a hugger."

"Um, sure."

Ms. Ann shuffled the few feet between them and wrapped her arms around Vivian in an embrace that brought tears to her eyes. *How did You know I needed this, Lord?*

"It's so nice to meet you, Vivian." The older woman pulled back. "I can't wait for you to fill my shoes. I've got a grandson I'm dying to get my hands on." She rubbed her palms together.

Vivian's heart turned over. She would have loved to have a grandmother around growing up. Then again, that would've been one more person filled with disappointment. Her actions had alienated her from her family, and now she'd face the Christmas season alone. Her throat ached at the thought, and she wrapped her arms around her middle.

"Should we go inside?" Ms. Ann asked. "I'm about to freeze in this November air. You'd think it was the dead of winter with these frigid temps."

Michael chuckled. "Come on in. Let's get y'all warmed up. I can get you some coffee if you'd like."

"Oh, how about that apple cider your father made famous?"

A shadow passed through Michael's dark eyes. Vivian wondered what had happened to his father.

As they walked into the general store, Vivian gave a

discreet glance at the produce, packaged goods and even clothing displayed to her right.

"Ms. Dupre, would you like some cider as well?" His brows raised, a mug held up as he stood near a drink station.

"Uh, no, and please call me Vivian." Hard cider had been one of her vices before she'd gotten sober and found the grace of Jesus. No need to tempt herself.

"Ms. Ann, do you mind if I get Vivian settled before we talk?"

"Actually…" She tapped her pointed chin. "I think Vivian could help with this, too."

Help with what? Her heart skipped. "Excuse me?"

"Well, you'll be taking over my position, which gives you an eagle-eye view of the community." Ms. Ann rubbed her hands together. "Yes, I think this will be perfect, especially since this isn't a task for just one person."

"Uh, Ms. Ann," Michael interrupted, "want to clue us in?" He handed her a cup of apple cider.

She slapped her forehead. "Of course. I'm so sorry. I'm an external processor. Anywho, the Richards family came down with the flu. They were set to run the Christmas Wishes program this year and now can't. I need a replacement ASAP so we can get the giving started."

Vivian had so many questions. What was Christmas Wishes? How many were in the Richards family? And why did Ms. Ann think Vivian could be of use?

The older woman glanced at Vivian, then stopped talking and shook her head. "There I go again. Going a mile a minute, and you don't even have the fuel to keep up." She propped a hand on her ample hip. "Every year, the church collects money to make people's Christmas dreams come true. Folks can nominate someone they think is in need."

Oh. Viv's heart turned over at the compassion. Was everyone in Willow Springs so charitable, or was it simply a result of the season?

"Ms. Ann, I have the general store and the rentals to run," Michael stated. "I'm not sure I'm the best fit for Christmas Wishes this year."

Michael's gaze flicked to Vivian's, assessing. Probably deciding if she could handle such a task. She straightened her shoulders. Michael knew nothing of her background, so as far as he was concerned, why wouldn't a future church receptionist be useful in a Christmas project? Sure, her faith was a little newer than her sobriety. While she'd been sober for one hundred eighty-four days, she'd only been a Christian about four months. Still, she could pretend to be qualified in whatever Ms. Ann needed her help with. Prove that God's grace hadn't been wasted on her.

"That's why it's a two-person job." Ms. Ann threw her hands up in the air in a *come on* gesture. "You can show Vivian the beauty of Willow Springs and the people in it. You know there's nothing like an Arkansas Christmas. Besides, I would think your background would make you a shoo-in. Didn't you head the charity department at your old job?"

"I did, but..." Michael's voice trailed off.

"You've got the experience and, with Vivian's help, the full load won't fall on you," Ms. Ann added.

Vivian's gaze locked with his, and her breath caught. While she'd love to see the splendor of northwestern Arkansas, she had no desire to get close to any man. She needed to focus on herself, like her sponsor recommended. Kate said it was best to avoid romantic relationships for a year to prevent old habits from returning. Not that Viv was *interested,* but still. If she could avoid spending time with her new landlord and stay on the straight and narrow, all the better.

"I'd be happy to help, Ms. Ann," Vivian offered. "From what you've told me about my receptionist duties, I should be able to juggle the two."

"Perfect," Michael claimed, pressing his hands together in support. "There you go. Ms. Dupre is your man—uh, woman."

"Bless your heart, Vivian. I so appreciate your help. But if Michael Wood thinks he's getting out of being on the team, he's gonna be surprised." Ms. Ann placed her hands on her hips. "You two already live in close proximity to one another. It makes the most sense. Don't make me call the pastor, young man."

Michael rubbed the back of his neck. "Of course I'll help, Ms. Ann."

Her lips curved in an impish grin. "That's what I thought." She set her mug down, pulled a folder from her tote and placed it on the counter. "Here you go. All the info you need." She closed her bag and headed for the front door. "I'll see you tomorrow, Vivian."

Vivian waved, too stunned by the turn of events to say anything else. How had she gotten herself in this pickle? She raised her gaze to Michael's and breathed out a prayer. *Help.*

Michael Wood stared at the empty space the Springs' receptionist had occupied mere moments ago. *What just happened?*

His gaze shifted to his new tenant. She wore her hair in a slicked-back high ponytail, shifting with every slight movement. Vivian Dupre was petite with honeyed skin that made him notice how deep of a brown her eyes really were.

What are you doing? Don't gawk at her like that.

Something about her screamed danger and disruption to his orderly life. Exhibit A: already getting thrust into the Christmas Wishes project despite being the sole owner and operator of Willow Springs' only general store. No one really wanted to travel to Walmart unless they absolutely had to, since the drive could take over an hour, so he had a lot of foot traffic. Not to mention renting out tiny homes to those who wanted to explore the Buffalo National River or head on down to the Ozark Mountains.

If he had to coordinate with Vivian on how to get the townspeople's wishes fulfilled as well, he'd be even more busy than he already was. Nevertheless, grumbling about being in a position to help made him feel guilty, so he'd stop the pity party. Only thing he had to figure out was how trustworthy his new tenant was.

He'd learned his lesson when it came to women and trust. The fact that she was beautiful as well—well, he didn't know if that was a plus or a minus. Regardless, he wouldn't be a fool and go any further than noticing. His ex had burned him well enough the scars still smelled like ash.

Michael cleared his throat. "Let's get you situated. I've got the paperwork in my office." He led the way across the room and down a hall to the office.

The family quarters were above the general store. Well, his quarters. His sister Pippen went to the University of Arkansas and hadn't visited a single weekend despite being less than two hours away. His brother, Charles, worked as a nurse in a clinic in the heart of Willow Springs and owned a home there as well. His other sister, Jordan, had chosen Fayetteville as her residence. He wasn't actually sure of her current occupation, as it changed with the wind. Together they made the dream team—at least that's what Pop always called them.

He pulled a green folder from a stack on the corner of his desk, opened it and slid out a few papers. "Add your occupation and sign at the bottom, please."

Vivian did so, her signature a flourish of movement. He watched her dainty hands as she handed him the items.

Michael gulped. "The rentals are all behind the main house. It's where we have the most acreage. They're a mixture of short-term and long-term tenants, though I group the shorties to the left, so they don't disrupt y'all too much." He rose and motioned for her to follow him.

Vivian nodded, her black ponytail bouncing with the movement. "How many homes do you have total?"

Michael opened the screen door and stepped off the front porch, heading for the side of the house. "Twelve. I can't decide if we need more. If we do add some—" he shrugged "—I'll probably have to hire more help." But how could he expect anyone to fill those positions when his own brother and sisters didn't want them? And why did he keep saying *we*? Some wishful thinking that his siblings would join his endeavors?

With Pop no longer around, Michael had become the head of the family. He'd tried to bridge the gap between himself and his siblings, but they always seemed irritated with him. He swallowed, pushing his thoughts aside. Right now, what mattered most was getting Vivian settled and his life back in order—as much as he could now that Ms. Ann had dropped another item onto his already-full plate.

One that would take time and effort.

"Ever think of wrapping the porch all the way around?" Vivian asked.

"Mom wanted a back deck, but Pop never got around to it." The memory almost pulled a smile from him. *Almost.* He'd had time to get used to Mom's absence, as she had passed more than a decade ago, but Pop's still felt fresh. It would be the second Christmas without his smiling face.

"Do you run this place with your folks?" she asked.

Michael rubbed the back of his head, trying to figure out the quickest way to rip the bandage off. "Just me."

"Oh," she murmured.

The sound of the dumpster being shut rang out like a shot in the still of the day. Vivian yelped, swinging in a circle before she realized nothing was wrong. Michael slowed his steps, eyeing her cautiously. She'd been skittish, like a colt being fenced in for the first time, ever since he laid eyes on her. He sure hoped she wasn't afraid of the great outdoors and the creatures that roamed, because Willow Springs had plenty of that to go around. Which reminded him…

"Make sure you take your trash to the disposal." He pointed toward the source of the loud clang behind the tiny homes. "Raccoons will visit and hound us if you don't. The potential for bear sightings is rare at best, but still, keep the trash locked up."

Her eyes widened.

Great. Maybe he should have saved that detail for a little later.

"Thanks for the warning," she said.

Her soft voice held a Southern accent reminiscent of the wealthy, though she didn't look the part. The simple jeans and jacket gave a nod to the casual. In fact, he was pretty sure you could find similar clothing at the nearest superstore.

He stopped in front of the semicircle the twelve tiny homes formed, a fire pit in the center of the landscaped yard. The houses were all different in color and shape, giving the double-row makeshift cul-de-sac a hodgepodge feel, but he liked it. Brought the place more character than having the same cookie-cutter homes to rent. The flatbeds allowed him to move things around if necessary—like if he built more.

Tomorrow he'd get the Christmas lights up on the tiny homes. Decorating was the thing that reminded him most of Pop, helping him feel more connected to his father.

Michael pointed to the first home on the right. The one with a cedar front that made people think of log cabins, cozy nights and peace that only nature could bring. "That's you."

"It's adorable."

"Uh, thanks." Not the word he'd use, but he wanted her to like the pick, so it would have to do. "You're booked until the end of June. It's 265 square feet. You'll enter through the side of the house, not the end." He pointed to the yellow doorway situated in the middle of the length of the home. "When you step inside, you'll see a closet and a ladder to the loft that houses a queen-size bed. The living room's to your left on the main level, and the kitchen is to the right. Beyond the kitchen is the bathroom, complete with toilet and shower."

He'd already cleaned the place, washed the bedding and made sure the place was all prepared. But he kept those details to himself.

"Wow. All that's in there?" She stared at the home, an unreadable expression on her face.

Was she apprehensive? Many people wanted to try a

tiny home but soon found it wasn't for them. Others loved it. "Yes, ma'am. Go ahead and have a look through. I'll stay out here so you won't feel crowded."

The first time he had a renter, he'd foolishly gone in with the couple who had booked the place for a week. It had quickly become obvious that there wasn't enough room for three people to view the interior. At least, not strangers who didn't know if you were going to move left or right and would bump into you. Now Michael just described the amenities and let people explore at their leisure.

Vivian nodded and took the keys dangling from his forefinger. "It's already furnished, right?"

"Yes, ma'am. It's been cleaned as well." He pointed to the little front porch. "You've even got a couple of chairs outside if you want to get some fresh air."

"Is it okay if I leave my car up front?"

"Sure can. Plenty of space, since only four of the homes are occupied right now."

The summer crowd had long gone, and those who wanted to experience the fall foliage and enjoy the sunshine before cold descended were tucked back into their regular-size homes. Though soon the holiday crowd would begin to show. Willow Springs had a lot in the way of Christmas festivities.

He hoped the momentum would continue and keep him with customers year-round. When Pop died, Michael had discovered his father had taken out a reverse mortgage on the general store. Seemed Pop had needed the money to put Pippen through school. Turning part of the acreage behind the store into Simplicity Rentals had been Michael's idea for keeping the store and plot within the family. He hadn't had the heart to explain those details to his siblings, so he was on his own.

Each day, he followed a schedule for cleaning, maintenance, financial upkeep and whatever else popped up on his to-do list. *Like the Christmas Wishes project.*

Michael cleared his throat. "If you need anything, I'll be at the store."

She nodded. "Thanks."

He tipped an imaginary hat and rambled back to the front. Seemed odd how she'd gone quiet all of a sudden. Was she an introvert? Or just simply observing everything before she came to any conclusions? Worrying tended to make him withdraw so he could analyze a way out of any predicaments.

Like now. He needed to figure out how to steer clear of her. Though working on the task Ms. Ann gave them would make that difficult. Maybe, just maybe, they could communicate through email or text. Anything but face-to-face. Vivian Dupre was too pretty for his peace of mind, and he didn't trust himself to judge her character correctly. Not when the last woman he'd misjudged became one of the reasons he'd returned to Willow Springs.

Chapter Two

Eeeee eeeee eeeee!

Vivian shot up, disoriented as the sound blared through the loft. Rubbing her bleary eyes, she found the culprit and swiped the alarm-dismiss button on her cell. "Ugh," she moaned.

Last night had to have been the *worst* sleep of her life, which made no sense. She had a comfortable bed, a place all to herself and the freedom of the outdoors right outside her window. But she hadn't counted on the stark stillness of night to keep her from a restful sleep. She'd been so very aware of just how alone she was. Not to mention the unfamiliarity of her surroundings. If someone had told her she'd become used to and even miss the county jail's routine, she would've laughed. But counting sheep well into the thousands last night had proven her wrong.

Perhaps coffee would get her through the morning. Rolling onto her knees, Vivian crawled toward the loft ladder, then descended to the main floor. There was a K-cup machine in the galley kitchen and flavored coffee pods in the welcome basket Simplicity gifted their renters. The basket held tea and hot cocoa pods as well holiday-inspired flavors. Had Michael put them together?

She couldn't imagine his large hands tying the red ribbon into a bow atop the basket handle. She shrugged. Regardless, the items were a blessing, since she hadn't done any grocery shopping yet. She'd have to peruse the general store more thoroughly to ensure she had items to stock her refrigerator and pantry. Better than driving to the nearest superstore and risking someone seeing her blow into the ignition interlock device on her steering wheel.

Rustling sounded outside the kitchen window, and she gasped, jumping back. A moment later, a squirrel skittered up a tree. Vivian dropped her head into her hands. Why had she let her parole officer convince her northwest Arkansas would be the best place for her new life? She should've stayed in Little Rock. The population was large enough that she might not run into anyone from her past. Then again, she'd been a total chicken, too afraid to take the chance. Hence the desire to go along with Bradley's relocation plan.

Probably because her first year of sobriety was crucial. Removing herself from temptation was just as important as a believer surrounding herself with like-minded people to help her learn the ways of Christ. Surely working as the new church receptionist would keep her on the straight and narrow. Maybe facilitating the Christmas Wishes program would even help. *Which you need to talk to Michael about.*

But first, coffee. Going through the details of who did what and when could wait.

She rubbed her eyes, grabbed the full mug and headed outside. Fresh air and a view would remind her that no jail cell would ever enclose her again. God had redeemed her, and she'd accept the gift of a new life.

Vivian sank into the patio chair, glad she'd grabbed a

sweater on the way out. The general store shined brightly in the dawn sky, the white lights warm and inviting. Her heart sighed at the thought of all the Christmas decorations probably going up around town now that Thanksgiving had passed. She turned her gaze to the horizon and the frost-covered trees.

This right here was enough to remind her she'd been blessed. Even though rest had evaded her throughout the night, she hadn't experienced true fear. Not like the past six months sleeping in the county jail.

"You're up early."

Vivian yelped, her coffee cup flying in the air and landing at her feet, the contents soaking the edge of her pajama pants and spilling onto the earth. "No!" she cried. "That was my first cup and I'd barely taken a sip. How will I wake up now?" She looked up at Michael, who held his hands palms out as if he faced a wild animal.

Granted, without coffee she undoubtedly gave off a fierce edge.

"Didn't mean to startle you. Sorry 'bout that."

The words barely registered as Vivian stared down at the spilled drink, imagining another time, another place. One where a wine bottle had tumbled and stained the interior of her car. Her reaching for it. The unexpected impact as the airbags blew up in her face.

She blinked. "It's not a problem." It was her own fault. Her fault for chasing success and a lifestyle of intoxication that had earned her jail time and a restricted license in the state of Arkansas. She picked up the mug, her fingers trembling as the memories flashed through her mind.

"We've got coffee in the store if you need more," Michael offered.

Vivian aimed for a calm smile though her insides

shook enough to land her on the Richter scale. "I'm good. I have more pods inside." She pointed to the home behind her.

"Sleep okay?"

Were they really doing small talk? "The mattress was more comfortable than I'd anticipated." Almost *too* comfortable. She hadn't expected a tiny-house bed to rival that of a luxury hotel. Perhaps she just needed to adjust and stop thinking of the thin mattress at County.

A gentle grin covered Michael's face. *Whoa.* His whole countenance changed, softening his woodsman persona and chasing the severity away.

"Glad to hear that. We really want our long-term tenants to feel right at home."

Vivian pushed a lock of hair behind her ear. "Are there no rentals in town? No apartments?" She vaguely remembered asking Bradley that question, but he was an outsider and hadn't known everything about Willow Springs.

"No." Michael snorted. "This is Willow Springs. We don't have an influx of people moving in. Some people rent out their homes but most of the youth move away. The people who come in to town are visiting. They'll hit the trails and explore nature, not stay and build a life."

A note of bitterness tinged his words. She looked around, taking in the countryside, the peace. "But it's so beautiful."

"Agreed. Though living in the middle of nowhere isn't for everyone." He crossed his arms, nodding at her. "What made you relocate to our neck of the woods?"

Her breath shuddered. Why hadn't she thought of a response for when people asked? She licked her lips. "I wanted a change in scenery." Completely true. A winter landscape was a lot better than steel bars in her face every day.

"Where you from originally?"

"Little Rock." A safe question to answer. What were the chances he knew someone down there who would know her?

Michael nodded. "Yeah, Willow Springs is a lot different. Pace out here is much slower."

"So, uh, should we discuss the Christmas Wishes program?" She tucked her arms under her armpits as the cold morning air began to seep through every gap in her ribbed sweater.

"Uh, yeah." He glanced at his watch. "What time do you have to be at the church?"

Right. It *was* Monday. "What time is it?"

"A quarter after seven."

"I have a couple of hours."

"Then if you want, I can make you breakfast, and we can discuss the program."

Eat breakfast together? Meals weren't included in the rental, though she'd yet to buy groceries. Not to mention while the old romantic in her immediately jumped to an idyllic picture, the jaded part of her brain shook the romantic side, reminding her she'd been sharing meals with others the past six months. Granted, Michael probably wouldn't serve her slop on a tray.

"Um, okay. I still need to do some shopping, so breakfast would be great."

"I'll get you a cup of coffee going as well."

She offered a stiff smile. "Appreciate it."

He dipped his head and headed back toward the farmhouse, leaving her wondering why he'd originally stopped by. Had it just been Christmas Wishes or something else?

Vivian headed inside to dress. Hopefully, her new wardrobe would look respectable enough for her new job. She picked out a pair of black slacks, a pale pink sleeveless top and a cream-colored cardigan. A quick brush of her shoulder-length black hair and a plain pink hair clip to pull the right side of it away from her face completed the look. Her hands shook as she opened a pack of foundation. When was the last time she'd worn makeup? Was that something Christian women did? She snapped the case closed and reached for her lip gloss instead. She didn't recall seeing Ms. Ann with any on. Maybe after attending church service, she'd come to a better conclusion.

She grabbed her coat and purse. The Bible she'd received in jail had the words *God Sets You Free* on the cover, so she'd bought a plain one when she'd updated her wardrobe. Now the plain black Bible rested in her bag along with a pen and the prepaid cell phone she'd purchased.

"Time to get back to the real world, Viv."

Michael put the biscuits on the plates, then grabbed the dishes. He'd already placed two cups of coffee in his office—just needed to bring the breakfast there. His feet came to a stop as the door opened and Vivian strolled in. Her professional look had his mouth drying out. He wanted to press a hand to his eyes and remind himself she couldn't be trusted. Or could she?

He used to pride himself on being able to discern whether a person had good character. After Alicia's betrayal, his judgment meter had been broken beyond repair.

All you gotta do is make it through the meeting, Mikey boy.

The more he remembered the wounds his ex had inflicted, the easier it would be to keep Vivian in the *do not engage* category. They could work together without developing a relationship that would lead to him calling her friend or adding the *girl* modifier.

"Hey, I've got breakfast." *Duh.* Could he sound any more foolish?

"Great. I can grab a plate." Her petite steps ate up the distance between them, and she took a dish.

"Thanks. We'll eat in the office."

Vivian nodded. No ponytail today. Just long black hair that brushed her shoulders and—

It didn't matter. He stalked away. *Lord, I don't know what's wrong with me. I've seen pretty women before. Why am I noticing her? Being with Alicia should have fried my attraction sensors.* He couldn't even think his ex's name without feeling resentment and bitterness welling up inside.

Michael sat and gestured for Vivian to follow suit. He reached for the folder Ms. Ann had left them with.

"So—"

"Could we—"

Michael nodded for Vivian to continue as the awkwardness of talking at the same time filled the air.

"Um, I was going to ask if we could say grace," she asked softly.

"Right. Sorry." He'd been about to break into full instruction mode, not bless his food. *Focus.* "Do you want to do the honors?"

Her eyes widened.

"Or not. I can say grace."

"Please."

Michael bowed his head. "Lord, thank You for this food. May it fuel us for the day. Amen." He resisted the urge to fidget. Praying out loud wasn't his thing, but he could tell that Vivian was more uncomfortable with the idea than he.

After they ate a few bites, Vivian wiped her mouth and spoke. "So, tell me all about Christmas Wishes."

Michael nodded. "The church has done the program for as long as I can remember. Throughout fall, people nominate others in need by submitting a name via the mystery box."

"Mystery box?" she asked.

"Yes." Michael took a bite of his biscuit before continuing. "There are a couple of boxes placed in the church for someone to drop a slip of paper with a name of the person and their wish. Everyone knows you're not guaranteed to be a Christmas Wish recipient. People like the anticipation of finding out who's being gifted regardless."

"Since Ms. Ann picked us to run it, does that mean we'll pick who gets their wish fulfilled?"

"Exactly. I looked over the paperwork last night. She's typed up everyone who was nominated and their need. She even put personal info, like if the person is a widower or single, etc."

A thoughtful look crossed Vivian's face. "How do we choose?"

"The church sets finances aside and the allotted amount helps determine who we'll choose. If we see a need that needs the whole amount, we can pick that person. Or we can pick five recipients and divide the amount. We're the deciding factor." He wanted to pop an antacid at the responsibility they faced.

Her face fell, lines framing her mouth. "That's…kind of sad."

"Agreed. This year, we have five thousand dollars to work with so that should hopefully fulfill a lot of wishes." *Please, Lord.*

"Could we add to the fund? Are there rules against that?"

He sat back, his mind buzzing. She wanted to *donate*? He hadn't seen that coming. Proof he didn't know what was what when it came to another's inner workings. *You don't even know her. You* knew *Alicia, though.*

"Michael?"

He blinked, focusing on Vivian. "Sorry. Um, I don't see a reason why we couldn't. Maybe check with Ms. Ann when you see her today?"

She nodded, glancing at the simple band on her wrist. Not a Fitbit or Apple brand in sight. Nothing but a plain black watch.

Vivian Dupre was a conundrum. Something about her screamed class, but her outward appearance stated she liked simple things. Which was the truth? The surface appearance—or the niggling feeling that raised the hairs on the back of his neck that said there was more than she showed?

"I'll do that." She took a sip of her coffee. "Could I take the folder and read it over? Maybe we can discuss this more tonight?"

Not if he could help it. Seeing her once in a day was fine. Besides, he'd promised to eat dinner with his brother. "I actually have plans."

"Oh. Of course." She blinked, her dark brown eyes watching him.

"Maybe tomorrow? I could make breakfast again?"

Her eyelids fluttered. "I can make my own, but we can certainly meet up again. Maybe at eight?"

"I'll be here."

She stood. "Thanks for the meal. I appreciate it."

"Sure. By the way, the store closes at seven. If you need anything, stop by before then."

"Oh, okay. What time do you officially open?"

"Nine." He rubbed the back of his neck. "I close from

eleven to two. Gives me time to have lunch and work on any rental business."

She nodded, a soft smile curving her lips. "Have a good day, Michael."

"You, too, Vivian."

Michael watched as she left his office. If only he could figure her out.

He shook off his musings and gathered the dishes. He'd wash them in his kitchen upstairs before opening the store. Already his to-do list had grown lengthy with items to cross off. Last night his rental notification had dinged, informing him he'd have two new guests this week. One would arrive today and the other on Friday.

After Pop passed, Michael had waffled with the idea of moving back home. Living in Bentonville and working for corporate America had been a dream. Then the fiasco with Alicia had exploded at work, making the decision easy for him. Only he'd never imagined he'd be here, running the place alone. Not a single peep or offer to assist him from Jordan or Pippen. Of course, he hadn't imagined his brother dropping his career as a registered nurse. Still, no one could be bothered to make family decisions together. They all nominated him to take over and trusted him to make the right choices. He rarely saw them now.

Did the desire for a better relationship with his siblings make him needy?

He sure was sappy this morning. He placed the dirty plates in the sink as his cell buzzed in his back pocket.

Chuck flashed on the caller ID.

"Hey, bro. What's up?"

Charles—or Chuck, as his brother was known by family—rarely called. Well, okay, Michael rarely phoned him, either. They usually communicated via texts.

"You still have the chain saw?"

Michael raised a brow. "Yes. Why? What's up?"

"Tree fell down on Spring Street. The sheriff is rounding up men who can help move it. I told him you had a chain saw."

Half the citizens of Willow Springs owned chain saws. Maybe this was Chuck's way of bridging the gap. "I'll be right there. Do you know if it's blocking the church?"

Had Vivian been able to get there safely? *Why do you care? She's just a tenant.* He huffed.

"Nah, it's a block away."

"All right. Be there in a few."

"Thanks, Mike."

Michael hung up, put the Be Back Soon sign up and locked the store. He headed for the tool shed. Unsure how bad the damage was, he grabbed rope, a lever and a pair of gloves. He placed the items in his 4x4 and a few miles later turned onto Spring Street.

A few vehicles hugged the shoulder, hazard lights blinking. He didn't see Chuck's blue SUV, so he parked and hopped out.

"Big Mike, thanks for coming out." Sheriff Rawley clapped him on the back.

"Hey, Sheriff. Brought some tools." He motioned to the back.

"Fantastic. Your brother told us you had the perfect shed at the homestead."

"I do. You never know what you'll need." Michael had discovered that while overseeing the building of the tiny homes last year.

"Ain't that the truth. Appreciate you jumping right in."

Michael nodded. Of course he would. That was the Willow Springs way. Nothing said Christmas spirit like joining in to ensure the citizens remained safe and could navigate the roads with ease. He just wished the rest of life could be that easy.

Chapter Three

Throughout her day, Vivian pored over the Christmas Wishes nominees. Ms. Ann had included information about each person's needs. However, the knowledge didn't make choosing any easier. Vivian didn't want to pick the wrong person. Which was probably why Ms. Ann had assigned two individuals to handle the program this year. Maybe Michael had a better idea of who would be the right choice, because Vivian didn't know anyone on the list.

She logged off her desktop and stood. Her receptionist duties were relatively light at the moment and definitely something she could handle. She prayed that this move had been the right step. That she hadn't taken the coward's way out by coming to Willow Springs instead of staying in Little Rock.

"Leaving for the day?" Ms. Ann asked.

"Yes, ma'am. Thought I'd check out the Sassy Spoon." She still couldn't believe someone had named a restaurant that.

"Oh, you'll love Ma Spooner's cooking." Ms. Ann grinned.

Was the owner really named Spooner? If so, that made the restaurant's name all the more engaging.

"I'm going home to do more packing."

Ms. Ann had told Vivian how she and her husband were moving to Tulsa, where her daughter and son-in-law lived. She had it worked out so she'd be finished packing by the time Vivian was trained in all things church related.

"Have a good evening," Vivian said.

"You, too, sweetie. Enjoy your meal."

She nodded, then left the office. How was she supposed to enjoy a meal alone? Being in county jail for six months meant Vivian hadn't eaten by herself in a while. Still, she'd felt very isolated those first few months in County as she had sobered up and started seeking more in life. She'd tried to keep her head down, mind her own business and not aggravate anyone. When County released her for time served, Vivian had left with a single friend from her experience. Billie—who'd been convicted of theft—had promised to keep in touch.

They'd met in Bible study and had accepted their need of a savior within a week of each other. Billie ended up being Vivian's lunch buddy and attended the jail's church services with her. Vivian's friend still had a few more months to serve before she'd be released. Until then, Vivian had promised to email her and send the occasional care package.

Vivian stared at her hatchback in the church parking lot. Having a restricted license meant she could drive to and from work, and to and from AA meetings. It also meant she shouldn't risk driving to the Sassy Spoon. A quick look on her phone's map app showed walking to the diner was completely feasible. After dinner, she could walk back to the church and drive to her tiny house.

Bonus, she wouldn't have to worry about anyone seeing her use the ignition device.

Decision made, Vivian went left. Something about Willow Springs eased the tension in her shoulders. The stone sidewalk gave the downtown area a quaint feel, as did the stone buildings. Occasionally a Victorian home stood in the midst of the businesses, some appearing to have been converted to shops. Wreaths hung from the streetlights, and a few businesses had been outfitted with colorful lights. She'd have to come back on the weekend and explore, meet the people in town. God willing, she'd make a friend or two.

Her mind turned to Michael. What was his story? Not that she particularly cared. She'd already made a promise not to get involved past the tenant-landlord relationship. Yet there was a darkness in his eyes that spoke of a heavy burden, which intrigued her. Maybe he hadn't learned how good the Lord was at carrying those problems too difficult for human arms.

As the businesses gave way to a stretch of wide open spaces, a log cabin came into view a little up the hill. A silver spoon had been attached to the roof with the word *Sassy* crossing it. The cedar wood had been outfitted with colorful Christmas lights, blinking in the dusk. As Vivian drew closer, the gold ornaments on the wreath hanging on the door came into view. A neon Open sign hung from the window next to a dancing snowman.

She opened the door, and Christmas music spilled out, the sounds of laughter and chatter its accompaniment. Her heart warmed at the sight, at the same time as her head reminded her of her solo status. She couldn't even call her parents to wish them happy holidays. One arrest—okay, so she'd had multiple opportunities to sober up and stay off the roads when intoxicated—and they'd cut her off. Told her not to call or show her face again.

Despite their warnings, Vivian had written to them after a month of sobriety. Her letter had gone unanswered, and her visitor list remained empty. When she accepted Christ as her savior, another letter had been sent and ignored. She shouldn't be too surprised, but that didn't negate the hurt.

She swallowed, shoving the pity-party thoughts out of her mind. A sign near the entrance told her she could seat herself. Her gaze stopped as it homed in on Michael and another man sharing a booth. Before she could avert her eyes, the other man turned and waved her forward. Mouth dry, she maneuvered between the tables toward theirs.

A few people turned curious eyes her way. She dipped her head in acknowledgment but forged ahead until she stood by Michael.

"Hi," she said breathlessly.

"Evening. Workday over?" His brow furrowed.

She nodded. Was he sorry his friend had waved her over?

"Um, Chuck, this is Vivian. She's new to Willow Springs, taking over Ms. Ann's position." Michael motioned to the other man. "Vivian, this is my brother. He's an RN at the local clinic."

Brother, not friend. "Nice to meet you," she murmured, glancing at Chuck. He wore a beard just like Michael, but everything about him seemed…smaller. Not in a negative way, just more calming. If she had to register him on the looks scale, she'd mark handsome, but not with the same impact as Michael.

But we're not taking note of that, are we, Viv?

"Likewise." Chuck proffered a hand, which she shook. "Welcome to Willow Springs. Why don't you join us?"

"Oh, no." Her cheeks heated. "I couldn't."

"I insist," Chuck said.

She peeked at Michael, who nodded, then slid over in the booth. Sitting next to him was the last thing she wanted, but she didn't want to be rude, either. Something about Michael Wood tugged at her heart strings. Instead of sharing that, she sat, said a quick prayer and proceeded to pick up the menu to hide behind. *At least this won't be the most awkward meal you've sat at.*

Apparently, the nudge of his foot hadn't been enough clue for Chuck to hop off the welcome wagon and leave his tenant alone. Now Michael had the uncomfortable feeling of sitting next to a woman he wanted to maintain distance from outside of anything related to Christmas Wishes and Simplicity Rentals.

"I hope you don't think I'm a bother," Vivian said.

"Not at all. We'll even buy you dinner as a welcome to town." Chuck smiled, his eyes flashing with amusement as he looked at Michael.

He got the message. *Michael* would be paying for dinner, *not* Chuck.

Michael nudged Chuck again out of spite, but his brother simply tossed a smirk his way. They used to be so close to each other, despite Jordan falling between them in lineup of oldest to youngest. Jordan's status as a girl had cemented Michael and Chuck's relationship. As they grew older, the distance widened. With Pop's death, it seemed a chasm too big to cross. The dream team—all of them named after basketball players—had fractured. Despite that, Michael was determined to resolve their issue. Whatever mystery problem that was.

"What's good?" Vivian asked.

"Everything," Chuck said.

Michael perused the items on his menu, then gave an inward shake of his head. He always got a burger, no matter how good the specials were or what else the restaurant offered. When you found a favorite dish, why try something different?

Vivian's eyes scanned the menu, and she licked her lips. "I think I'll have the potpie."

"Great choice." Chuck grinned. "You can't go wrong with any of the food. Ma Spooner is a great cook."

Michael wanted to disagree on principle. He didn't know what his brother was up to, but something was off. Michael tapped the table, hoping Chuck would notice and look his way, but no, his brother's gaze stayed on Vivian, who shifted slightly next to Michael. He couldn't help but note the slight dip in the booth.

"Do y'all eat here often?" she asked.

"Everyone does." Michael spoke before thinking. Feeling heat rising up his neck, he motioned toward the crowd. Every table was full. "Ma's a good cook. If you're not cooking at home, you're at the Sassy Spoon."

"Truth," Chuck agreed. "I eat here almost every night. I'm not a big fan of cooking."

"I'm usually too tired after working at the store," Michael added. Not that Vivian probably cared.

"You know what," Chuck said slowly, "I just realized I've got leftovers in the fridge. I should leave. Can't let that go to waste."

Michael's back stiffened. "You could have it for lunch tomorrow." He stared his brother down, hoping he'd hear Michael's unspoken plea to stay. No way did he want to sit with Vivian alone.

"Another time. It was nice meeting you, Vivian." Chuck tossed a wave and left the booth.

Silence descended at the table, magnifying the background noises coming from the kitchen and the other patrons. Michael couldn't believe it. What happened to the olive branch of having dinner with his brother? Just like Chuck to leave at the first opportunity of escape.

Vivian jumped up from beside him.

"Wait, you're leaving, too?" The words flew from his lips, and he wanted to snatch them back.

Her mouth dropped open. "No. I was just going to move across from you. I was trying to avoid the awkwardness."

"I think any time you witness some family tension, comfort goes right out the window."

"I'm sorry," she whispered, sitting back down next to him.

"It's not your fault." Michael tossed his hands in the air. "Though I'm not rightly sure whose fault it is. We just don't…mesh." His hands landed atop his head as he rubbed the back of it.

"I'm sure the problem will correct itself."

He could only hope. "From your lips to God's ears."

Her lips curved. "I used to hate that saying when I was young, but now it makes me happy."

"Why's that?" He turned and eyed her.

"Because I know God's listening. Even before we realize it."

Michael nodded slowly. "You're right. That's something I often forget." It was why prayer wasn't his first reaction to solving a problem. Maybe if it was, he wouldn't have let Alicia get away with corporate espionage.

"It's something I'm just realizing."

"Baby Christian?" he asked, hoping he sounded merely curious.

Her brows lowered, and she looked down at the table. "It shows?"

"Not at all. Your last comment made me suspect."

Kristin came by and took their orders, then headed back toward the kitchen area.

"Um, I'm going to move across from you."

"Oh, right." He barely hid a sigh of relief as the space widened between them. Now he didn't have to notice the honeyed smell of her perfume, shampoo or whatever created the intriguing fragrance.

Silence enveloped them once more as Michael scrambled for something to break the lull.

"I looked over the nominees," Vivian stated.

"Yeah?" He leaned forward, glad she'd brought up a topic he had thoughts on. "What did you think?"

Before she could answer, the Sassy Spoon's owner came up with their food.

"Thanks." Michael grinned up at her as Vivian echoed the sentiments.

"Anytime, hon." The woman extended a hand to his new tenant. "I'm Ma Spooner. My daughter, Ree, is in the kitchen whipping up more food. If you need anything else, let me know. Ya hear?"

"I will."

Ma Spooner slapped Michael's back. "Eat up, Big Mike, and next time tell Chuck to stick around."

He chuckled. "Yes, ma'am."

"Everyone seems really nice," Vivian stated once they were alone.

"We like to welcome people, especially since most of them are tourists. We want repeat business." He motioned to her food. "Mind if I say grace?"

"Please."

He bowed his head, thanking God for their food and the company. His voice faltered as he realized the truth of it. He *was* thankful for her company. It didn't have to mean anything momentous. Simply that he wasn't eating alone.

Her *amen* pulled him out of his spiral, and his head snapped up.

"I'm still not used to doing that in public," Vivian admitted.

"How long have you been a believer?" he asked. Hopefully that was the polite thing to ask.

"Four months." Her lips curved in a smile that held so much peace he almost gaped.

Almost. Because even though she was opening up about her faith, part of him heard warning bells. Why four months? What had happened to make the change? Not that it was any of his business.

He swallowed. "That's awesome. What made you believe?" Oops. That question slipped out.

She bit her lip. "I wanted to believe His grace was really unfathomable, so I asked Him to help my unbelief. The rest is history."

He bit into his burger. Would God's grace keep him from feeling like a fool? Why hadn't he fallen to his knees before God when Alicia told their boss the ideas she'd submitted were her own? Why hadn't he done something…*anything*?

"I'm happy for you," he said around the ache in his throat.

"Thank you. What about you? How long have you been a…believer?"

"Birth." At least that's what Pop used to say. "I don't really have a conversion story. I've just always believed." His face heated. Did he sound pretentious?

"I like that," she said softly. "Do you know if all those on the Christmas Wishes list are believers?"

He shook his head. "It's not a requirement. It's the

church's hope that we'll reach all the townspeople, not just the ones that go to the Springs."

"Wow. With a ministry like that, maybe they'll change the heart of a nonbeliever." She dipped her silverware in her potpie. "How are we supposed to pick?"

"Prayer. Sharing if we think someone should be a recipient. I'm sure there are people we'll agree on."

She nodded slowly. "What about Jimmie?"

"Jimmie?"

"The kid who hasn't been out of the house in a year because he's immunocompromised? He asked for a gaming chair, a desk and a laptop to continue his online learning."

Michael snapped his fingers. "He's a fifth grader, right?"

"Yes." She nodded her head enthusiastically.

Huh. He sat back, surprised. "How did you remember his name?"

"I've been reading the names and their bios all day. When I got to the end of the list, I reread from the top."

Michael had spared it a quick glance. Certainly hadn't pored over the contents enough to memorize everyone.

"I was kind of hoping to get your take on the people. I figured you know all those listed."

Willow Springs was small enough for that to be possible. But he'd have to think hard to pinpoint who had a kid that lived inside because of a chronic illness. "I'm not sure I recall meeting a Jimmie."

"Makes sense if he can't leave the house."

"Yeah, but that makes me wonder about his parents."

"Oh, that's easy," Vivian said. "The dad works at the local Walmart and the mom does online tutoring."

"There is no local Walmart."

She frowned. "I thought the notes said that."

"Probably, but the nearest one is about an hour's drive away."

"Poor guy."

"Let's make him our first recipient, then. How much could all of that cost, anyhow?"

Vivian shook her head, amusement twitching her lips. "Gaming chairs can cost hundreds of dollars alone. Ms. Ann did say we can add to the fund. So maybe we just get him a laptop."

He blew out a breath. "We're definitely going to need lots of prayers, then. It's the only way we can pick the right people."

Vivian rested her chin in her hands. "Then praying it is."

Michael could only hope he wouldn't feel guilt over anyone who didn't get chosen for the project.

Chapter Four

Vivian shook out her hands as she walked the distance from her tiny home to the general store. Throughout her morning preparations, a nervousness had clung to her like wax on a fly trap. Before she'd slept last night—a sleep not much better than the first night in her new home—she'd prayed to God for wisdom over the Christmas Wishes nominees. She didn't know who everyone was, didn't know their backstories or their struggles, but trusting that God was in the details kept her from spiraling.

Her strain this morning could probably be attributed to her meeting with Michael. Something about him put her on edge. Not the kind she'd experienced being in County for six months. Getting sober, keeping her head down, adhering to the rules and trying to make sure she didn't become a target had stressed her to the max and were the reasons she still looked over her shoulder. That tension wasn't the same type she had around Michael. Unfortunately, she couldn't put a word to the emotions crowding her mind now.

She went through some relaxation techniques, repeated Bible verses to bring her peace and shook her hands all the way to the front door of the general store, as if water droplets would fall off her fingertips. It was only eight o'clock and the store hadn't officially opened yet.

Vivian peeked through the paneled glass, looking for her landlord. Should she knock? Wasn't like there was a doorbell to ring. Or maybe the door was unlocked. She reached for it, then froze. What if it *was* unlocked but Michael didn't want anyone coming inside yet and called the cops because he thought her an intruder? She gulped and rapped her knuckles on the door instead. Hopefully the sound carried.

She almost jumped when Michael's tall frame shadowed the glass. Instead, she stepped back and slid her hands into her jacket pockets. The thin windbreaker material was no match for the dipping temperatures. She couldn't remember a chill this cold in winters past.

"Morning, Vivian."

Michael's deep voice had her bobbing her head in response. Her cheeks heated at her silliness, and she cleared her throat. "Good morning."

He raised a pointed eyebrow at her coat. "You might need something thicker."

"It's all I have."

"Well, look around. The store isn't officially open, but I have no problem getting you into something warmer."

Vivian's eyes met his. He seemed more relaxed today than yesterday. Why couldn't she be?

"Do you want to?"

"Um, excuse me?"

"Get a new jacket?" He pointed over his shoulder to a circular rack that held warm outerwear.

"Yes, please." She rushed across the room and started sifting through the options. Some were flannel, while others were quilted.

She pulled out a black quilted jacket. "Is it okay if I try it on?"

"Of course." He shuffled away.

Vivian slid off her windbreaker and put the jacket on. Instantly the chill that had weeded its way through her skin left. She sighed. "I'll take it."

Wait, she'd forgotten to check the price. Fortunately, she still had a paycheck from before she was incarcerated sitting in her checking account. Ms. Ann had said she'd get paid in three weeks, so Vivian needed to be smart with her funds. Her savings account had been wiped out by the fine she'd received along with her sentence.

A breath escaped her lips when she noted the reasonable amount on the tag dangling from the sleeve. She shrugged off the jacket and headed for the counter where Michael stood.

"Thanks again for this."

"Sure thing. Don't forget to buy stuff to fill up that fridge."

She smiled. "Yeah, I plan on doing that after work." Once she figured out what she wanted to eat. Freedom to choose left her strangely overwhelmed.

"Or, of course, you could always frequent the Sassy Spoon."

"Do they do breakfast? I didn't catch the hours."

Michael nodded. "The Spooners open earlier and stay open a little later than everyone else. Seven to nine. Just flip the numbers to remember."

"Oh good." But also a little strange. What did people do if they needed that last minute item and stores were closed? Did people truly borrow sugar from their neighbors?

"It is. Since the town doesn't keep city hours, we're

forced to relax. The townsfolk can all attend a Friday night football game or Saturday basketball event."

"Local teams?"

"Yes. Though occasionally Ma Spooner opens the diner for late games if it means watching the Razorbacks."

Vivian bit back a smile. Arkansans did have a deep-abiding love for all things Razorbacks. She stuffed the receipt Michael passed to her into her new coat pocket. "Should we get down to business?"

Michael nodded. "Want to head to my office or should we chat out here?"

"Whatever's easiest."

Out here gave her more space to breathe, but she didn't want him to notice her discomfort in small spaces, either. Plus, what better way to overcome than to deal with it?

"Office, then."

Vivian swallowed but followed him. She shook out her hands a few times then stuffed them back into her pants pockets.

"I was thinking last night," Michael started as he took a seat. "What if we covertly observed the nominees?"

"Stalk them?" She couldn't help the rise in her voice at his absurd suggestion. They couldn't just watch Willow Springs citizens. That was…creepy.

He grimaced. "Not stalk. That's a heavy connotation and not what we're doing. We simply want to observe."

"Isn't that passing judgment, though? Trying to figure out who's more deserving?"

"That is what Ms. Ann asked of us. How else are we supposed to know who to help?"

Vivian blew out a breath and sat back in her seat. "I don't know, but I draw the line at that." She didn't need the cops called on her because Michael wanted to *observe* people.

"Fine. Bad idea."

You think? She clamped her teeth together.

Michael blew out a breath, running a hand down his face. His beard, trimmed close and neat, made Vivian wonder if he snipped the hairs daily. *Get your head out of the clouds.*

She stared down at her hands, thoughts searching for any idea of how to proceed. "Okay, how many nominees do we have?"

He opened the folder and peeked at the list. "Fifty."

"Is it possible to meet all their needs while spending a hundred dollars on each of them?"

Michael groaned. "Not at all. Jimmie alone is asking for a whole desk setup."

"Is there anything that says we can't get outside help?"

"What do you mean?" He leaned forward.

Vivian's heart rate ticked up as excitement coursed through her. "What if we ask some of the local businesses to donate items? If there's a place in Willow Springs that can donate even one item that would fulfill a wish, then we'd have money left over for the more expensive requests."

"That's a great idea." Michael's eyebrows rose. He scanned the list again, eyes moving slower as if assessing the needs. "Really good. One of the nominees needs a crib. Apparently, they just had a home built for them through Habitat for Humanity. Now they need furnishings for a baby."

"You know someone who could donate a crib?"

He nodded. "Yeah. Fiona runs a store geared toward the ages of newborn to preschool, I believe."

"That's fantastic!" She scooted to the edge of her seat.

"If you want to take the names of those you think we can get donations for, then I can work at pricing out the others. Maybe we can make all their Christmas wishes come true."

A tiny part of her—okay, a bigger portion than she wanted to admit—wanted to have one of her dreams granted. One that involved her parents around the fireplace with the Christmas tree decorated in all its splendor. Christmas was one of her mother's favorite holidays, and she always went all out decorating the house. Vivian could practically imagine their large home with a wreath hanging from each window. Garland draped around the entryway. Not to mention the white lights her mother always hired someone to hang.

"Vivian?"

She blinked, Michael's form coming into focus. "I'm sorry. What did you say?"

"I printed off a copy after highlighting the names I'll handle."

"Great." She took the proffered sheet and stood. "Then we'll touch base this evening when I shop for groceries."

"Yeah, that sounds great."

She nodded and waved goodbye, relieved the meeting hadn't been long and that the uneasy feeling that had woken her up had abated. Perhaps being around Michael Wood wouldn't upset her delicate sensibilities. She snorted and headed for her car.

Michael rested his forehead in his hands, thankful that no one was in the store at the moment. Added blessing—no one had a rental issue. Early today, he'd been running around seeing to everyone's needs. The forecast called for freezing rain tonight, which had people stopping in all day to buy food and items to help keep them warm.

Then one of the toilets went on the fritz on the shortie side of Simplicity Rentals. He'd whispered a prayer of thanks when he finally got it up and running.

After all that business, his lunch break had almost ended, but not before he'd managed to grab a PB&J. Now he had about two more hours before he could flip the Open sign to Closed. Until then, he was hiding out on the stairwell leading to his apartment. It was the perfect place to hear the phone ring in his office or the door chime if someone entered the store.

Ding.

He muffled a groan, head falling back in exhaustion. Why were so many people pulling at him today? He chided himself for ever thinking his pop had had it easy running the store. It was one reason Michael had added the tiny homes to the family acreage. Pop had handled the general store with ease, and Michael had never seen him complain. Now that he was older and had worked multiple jobs, Michael could admit that Pop just probably hid that side of himself.

Slowly, Michael stood and walked around the hidden partition. He froze at the sight of Vivian. Was it truly time for her to be off work? Not that he'd been paying attention to her hours, but he'd assumed she'd be by closer to six.

"Hey, Vivian."

She dipped her head, then he noticed the phone attached to her ear. He couldn't make out the conversation. Judging by the furrowed brow, someone had a lot to say, preventing her from talking.

What was her story? What made a person leave Little Rock and come to Willow Springs? Being sandwiched between the Buffalo National River and the Ozarks meant the town was rural even with a day full of tourists. Granted, some people did want a slower pace of life.

He supposed Vivian could be one of those, but something in his gut said that was unlikely.

What do you know? Your character meter needs to be recalibrated.

Michael sighed and meandered toward the counter. Vivian would speak to him whenever she was off the phone. Of that, he was sure. Because if she didn't initiate a conversation, he would. He'd been surprised by how many businesses were willing to donate to Christmas Wishes—the ones he'd reached out to before business picked up—most with the prerequisite that he pick the items up himself. Made him thankful he owned a truck and not a small sedan like the one he'd seen Vivian drive up in the other day.

"Hey, there," Vivian said as she hung up her call and placed some items on the counter. "I didn't see a basket."

He pointed to the stand of baskets right beside the door.

"Oh, I didn't even look there." Her grin turned sheepish. "Is it okay if I leave these here while I grab a few more items?"

"Of course." He cleared his throat, waited a beat, then asked, "How'd you do with your list?"

"I made good headway in between the work Ms. Ann had for me." She came back holding jars of peanut butter and strawberry jam—his favorite.

"How are you liking the work?"

She tilted her head, brown eyes getting a faraway look. "You know, I like it." She straightened, meeting his gaze. "You? Do you like working here?"

"Most days."

Her grin quirked, a flash of white teeth attracting his attention. "Not today, huh?"

He let out a soft laugh. "Definitely not. However, I

did make headway with my portion of the list. Four businesses are willing to donate. I'll make more calls tomorrow and see if that number grows."

"Of course. I didn't expect either one of us to finish today."

Michael glanced at the calendar. "Tomorrow marks the beginning of December. We should plan for when we'll deliver the gifts."

Her eyebrows rose. "Deliver? I thought we would buy everything, wrap them and give them to the church."

"No, ma'am." He shook his head. "Part of the fun is delivering the packages to their residences. Sort of like ding-dong ditch, but with Christmas presents."

Vivian laughed, and the sound seemed to brighten the store. Michael blinked and began scanning her items. What was wrong with him? Noticing how she laughed? Wasn't that how Alicia had gotten her snares into him? A laugh here, empathy there, and before he knew it, they were dating seriously while she secreted his work information behind his back.

"That sounds fun."

"We should come up with a plan."

"Okay. Should we have breakfast at the Sassy Spoon tomorrow?"

He smoothed his face to cover the shock. She wasn't asking him on a date, right? *Of course not. It's all Christmas Wishes business.* Still, he couldn't ignore the part of him that broke out in a cold sweat at the idea of getting involved with another woman.

"Or not. I'm sure you're busy. I just wanted an opportunity to try their breakfast menu."

"No, that's fine." It'd have to be. The sooner they could get everything squared away, the better.

"All right then. See you there?"

"Yeah, um, seven? That way we both have time to get to our jobs afterward."

Vivian nodded. "Seven it is."

"Your total is fifty dollars and eighty cents. Do you need me to bag these, or did you bring any reusable ones, by chance?"

"Was I supposed to?" Her eyes widened in surprise.

"No, no. Some people do. But I can place them in paper or plastic."

"Paper is fine."

He quickly opened a paper bag and began stacking the jars at the bottom, adding the more squishable items to the top. "It won't be too heavy to carry, will it?"

She smirked. "Because I have such a long walk behind the store."

"Sorry." He bit back a chuckle.

"Nothing to apologize for. I'm too sarcastic for my own good at times."

"Oh, I can speak fluent sarcasm as well. I usually save it for conversations with my brother and sisters."

"How many sisters do you have?"

"Two."

"And just the one brother?"

He dipped his head.

"Bet you're the oldest."

He froze. "What makes you say that?" And why was he saying all this? It wasn't like him to just tell people his business.

"You have control issues written all over you." She slapped a hand to her mouth, eyes going wide. Then she slowly dropped her hand. "And I have no filter—only-child syndrome. I am so, *so* sorry."

"It's okay. Promise." But wow had she been scary accurate.

Her cheeks reddened, and she grabbed her bags.

"Promise. You didn't hurt my feelings."

"Good," she murmured. "See ya."

"Bright and early at the Spooners'."

She bobbed her head and hustled out the door. Michael sighed, resting his forearms on the counter. Before he could take a few deep, cleansing breaths and wonder why Vivian had shut down so quickly, the door chimed and more customers came in.

The last two hours sped by, and Michael finally flipped the Closed sign over. He wanted to pump his fist in the air and raise a hallelujah to the Lord. But first, he needed to clean up before making sure his to-do list for the rentals was complete for the day.

Half an hour later, he strode outside and shivered. He needed to make sure the faucets were trickling in the vacant properties and remind the others to let theirs drip. He really hoped the ice storm would turn and spare Willow Springs, but weather had begun to change over the last decade or so, and he didn't expect it to get any better.

For some reason, he left Vivian's property for last, still picturing her embarrassment at the humor she'd shown. She hadn't seemed self-conscious the day she'd arrived, just a little jumpy and quiet, but now he wondered if she had scars she was covering.

Don't we all?

He knocked on the door and waited.

A few seconds later, he heard shuffling then the latch unlocking.

"Hi. Sorry to bother you," he rushed out, so she'd know it was his issue and nothing on her part. "I forgot to let you know there's an ice storm coming through. If you would, make sure the faucets drip before going to sleep tonight. We don't want any frozen pipes."

"Of course. Thanks for letting me know."

"Sure thing. Have a good night."

"You, too." She quickly closed the door, and he heard her lock it.

Michael walked away, hands in pockets and thoughts focused on his new tenant. He didn't know her story, and even though part of him *wanted* to know, it was best for both of them if he kept his curiosity at bay.

Chapter Five

Ice glistened in the sunlight, turning Willow Springs into a frozen winter wonderland. Vivian exhaled, watching as her breath formed in the air and dissipated. Walking down Main Street had seemed like a smart choice at the time. She'd parked in the church's empty lot this morning then set out for the Sassy Spoon on foot. But the ice-covered sidewalks had her quickly moving to the grass to prevent falling on her backside. Part of her wondered if she'd have to come clean. Let the townspeople know she had a DWI on her record. It was becoming tiresome trying to hide her routine of blowing into the interlock device in order to get the car to start. Not to mention demoralizing.

When she'd informed her parole officer that she'd become a believer, his exact words had been "Good for you. Now keep that up on the outside." Not that Vivian could blame him. So many people claimed religion in the county jail just to get a little more free time out of their cells. Sitting in a spacious room used for church services ranked a lot better than being behind bars.

But for her, it had been real. That gut-deep knowledge that she'd been forgiven and could go forth a changed person had made sobriety in the outside world easier to manage. The yearning to numb her feelings wasn't as intense as it had been those first few months. While it was still present, today she knew God would get her through another day. Not on her own strength but His.

Vivian sniffed, nose tingling in the cold. She wanted to do a jig to warm up as the big spoon came into view. Instead, she scanned the lot for Michael's truck but didn't see the 4x4. Maybe he was still driving those few miles into town.

Her eyes adjusted to the light as she walked inside the Sassy Spoon and scanned the premises. Just as she found an empty booth, a man stopped a couple of feet away from her. She waited, wondering if he wanted to say something or if he would just stand there, his face turning as red as a tomato.

"Uh, I wanted to welcome you to Willow Springs, ma'am," the gentleman said, his accent just as Southern as biscuits and sausage gravy. His words were soft and a little bit hesitant.

"Thank you. I'm Vivian Dupre."

He nodded. "Mason Sanders. I, uh, run the Christmas tree farm on the outskirts of town."

There was a tree farm? Excitement zipped through her at the thought of a decorated tree. Wait, could she even fit a full-size evergreen in her tiny house? "That sounds wonderful."

His face reddened. "Yes, ma'am. It's what I've always known."

"I appreciate the warm welcome."

"Uh, wasn't much." He shifted his stance. "I, uh, actually wanted to talk to you about Christmas Wishes."

Vivian tensed. "What about it?"

"I nominated a person. And, uh, not sure if you've

read through them all yet, but I thought I'd make an extra effort to, uh, you know, get you to really consider my nomination."

"Who did you suggest?"

"Stacey, ma'am. She hasn't seen her family in years. Keeps getting hit in the wallet with expense after expense."

Who wouldn't want to be with family, especially this time of year? Vivian recalled the nomination, but there had been no extra details other than "needs to visit family." "Who hasn't she seen?"

Mason gulped. "Her mother and sisters. Her mother's health is failing, and she doesn't have the funds to travel."

"Oh, my," she murmured. Vivian couldn't imagine being in that position. She'd do anything to see her mom, get a hug from her and hear words of comfort.

"Thank you for telling me about Stacey. I'll be talking over everything with Michael."

"Big Mike's a good guy. I'll be praying for y'all."

"Thank you, Mason."

He nodded, tipped his hat and walked around her, maintaining a wide berth.

She blew out a breath and continued to the booth. A second later, Michael walked in, the bell chiming his arrival. She slipped off her jacket, thankful her back wasn't to the door.

"Sorry I'm late. One of the homes had a plumbing issue I had to see to."

"No worries. Everything squared away?"

"It is now." He rubbed his forehead. "FYI, rubber duckies belong in bathtubs and not toilets."

Vivian clamped her teeth over her lip to keep from laughing. Frustration came off Michael in waves, and she didn't want him thinking she was making light of his plight…despite how utterly hilarious it was. She could only imagine the look on his face when a toy popped up from the pipes.

She stared down at the table, rubbing her mouth to smother the chuckles bubbling up.

"Are you laughing at me?" he asked quietly.

Her head flew up, and she caught the humor glinting in his eyes. Her snicker flew free, and soon he joined her.

She pressed her hands to her cheeks. "I can only imagine the expression you must have had when you plunged out a rubber duckie."

"The tenant couldn't look me in the face."

"She probably didn't know her kid had flushed it."

Michael stared right into her eyes. "She doesn't have any kids."

Vivian's mouth opened, then her head dropped back, cackles escaping. A snort followed as she tried to calm herself. "Please tell me the culprit was a previous tenant." She wiped tears from her face.

"No can do."

"Oh, man." She gasped for breath.

"Thanks for laughing. I needed to let off some steam. And now I can see the humor."

"You're welcome?" She shrugged.

"Let's order." He waved a hand in the air, and a server came to their table.

After the server left, Vivian leaned forward to tell Michael about her conversation with Mason.

"That's rough. Stacey's a sweet person."

"You know her?" And how silly was that question? Willow Springs wasn't a sprawling metropolis.

"Yes. She's lived in Willow Springs about five years now."

"I remember seeing her name because I looked up the

cost for flights to…" she paused as she opened her notes, searching for Stacey's name "…Oklahoma."

"Expensive?"

"It's about five hundred round trip with taxes."

"Not terrible."

"No, totally doable. Plus, we'd still have money left over for the others."

Michael rubbed his beard. "Is that something we can get a discount on? See if an airline wants to participate in fulfilling a wish? Or at least get some kind of voucher so she can pick the travel dates?"

"We could certainly call and ask. Why don't you tell me what you found from the local businesses?"

While she ate biscuits with sausage gravy—*thanks for the idea, Mason*—and Michael chowed on pancakes, they discussed the ins and outs of the lists of contenders.

"I say we start with the Diaz family. The father lost his job, and the wife is a stay-at-home mom. They were nominated for groceries to stock their pantry."

"Are you going to donate food to them from your store?" Vivian paused, coffee mug in hand.

"Sort of. I thought I'd print off some vouchers allowing them so much money in groceries and then make a Christmas dinner basket we could drop off a few days before the holiday." He wiped his mouth. "What do you think?"

"It's brilliant." She could only imagine the relief that would bring. "Let's do it."

"All right then. I'll print off the vouchers, make a little booklet and then we can drop it off in their mailbox."

"I think that's illegal. Maybe put it in the screen door?"

Michael nodded.

"Oh! Should we take pictures discreetly and later on

do a slideshow for the church? Or is that weird?" It was weird. Creepy even, right?

An indecisive look filtered into Michael's eyes. "I'm not sure. They might not want their pictures posted. And it would probably be best to get their permission, if we even did do that."

"You're right. There's a reason nominations were anonymous." Vivian blew out a breath. She felt silly for suggesting something so harebrained. "I'm going to head to work now." She pulled out her wallet and grabbed a twenty, tucking it under the bill slip. "I put enough for my meal and some for the tip."

"Have a good day."

Vivian tensed at the farewell that sounded oddly intimate. Then she mentally berated herself. It was simple good manners to wish someone a good day. "Thanks. You, too." Still, her stomach tensed at the picture they made of sharing a meal and then sending each other off to face the day.

Shake it off, Vivian. Besides, no one in the diner spared them a second glance. So she would weave in and out of the tables and head to work like the morning had been perfectly normal.

Michael propped his feet up on his coffee table and exhaled. Today had been a long day. One of the tiny homes had had a pipe burst because the tenant failed to let the water drip like he'd cautioned everyone the day before. Despite the warning gurgling noise, he still tried to use the shower instead of notifying Michael of the issue. Then the rubber duckie incident followed. On top of that, he'd run out of apples and bananas and the next delivery wasn't scheduled until Saturday, when Paul would arrive with the new shipment of produce. Not to mention the upset customers Michael dealt with. Fortunately, he'd been able to talk them down. One asked for a refund—shortie tenant who believed the tiny home should have been bigger—and the other expected a refund on a T-shirt that had been too small for his wife.

Now all Michael wanted to do was stream a true crime episode and eat dinner. Though the thought of cooking a meal or even driving to the Sassy Spoon had him resting his head on the back of the couch in defeat.

His phone rang, making him jump in the stillness of his apartment. He pulled out his cell from his back pocket and looked at the caller ID.

Jordan flashed across the screen.

"Hey, Jay, what's up?"

"Hey, big brother. How's life treating you?"

He raised an eyebrow. Jordan always had a reason for calling. What was it this time? Something in her voice sounded off.

"Busy. It was one thing after the other all day long."

"What are you doing now?"

Did she really care or was she buttering him up for a big ask? "Dreaming of food and how I can get it in front of me without lifting a finger."

"Taste and see the Lord is good, brother dear. Doesn't the Bible teach us that man can't live on bread alone?"

Wow, were her words saturated in vinegar. "It does. But Jesus also took time to feed people's physical bodies and not just their spirits."

"Mmm."

"Everything okay?" He placed his feet on the floor and sat up, resting his elbows on his knees.

"As good as can be expected."

"Talk to me, Jordan. What's up?"

She blew out a breath, creating static over the line.

"Everything is falling apart out here. My roommates are upset with me."

"Why? I thought they were your besties." All three of them had left Willow Springs without a backward glance.

"A man. What else is capable of tearing a decade-old friendship apart?"

Michael struggled for the words. He didn't know what to say to comfort Jordan. He'd never heard her sound so bitter. "Are you okay?" he asked softly.

She sniffed. "I know I said I'd be back for Christmas and that was it, but could I…would it be possible to stay…*indefinitely*?"

"Of course. This is your home. You don't have to ask if you can return."

"I don't want to step on your toes. Wasn't sure if you're dating someone or whatnot."

Michael barely trapped the scoff from flying free. "No someone. Just me working 24/7."

"Then thanks. I'm not sure how much longer I'll be welcomed here."

"Say the word and I'll clean out your room."

"Don't do it just yet. Who knows, maybe things here will resolve. I just needed to know I have a fallback plan."

Michael had so many questions but wasn't sure if he should ask them. He wanted to know who had offended whom and what man had come between them and how. Had they all just developed a crush on the same guy, or was there more to the story?

Instead, he searched for a different talking point. "When do you think you'll be down for Christmas?"

"Probably a few days before, unless something changes here."

"All right. Can't wait to see you."

"Same, Mike."

"Call if something changes and you need to come home."

"Will do. I guess I'll talk to you later."

"Okay." He hated the awkwardness between them. Yet how did a person span the distance that seemed to grow each year?

They said their goodbyes, and Michael set his cell on the coffee table. He rested his face in his hands.

Pop had been the glue that kept the Wood family together. They'd been scattered in different parts of Arkansas, but upon his passing, the four siblings had permanently gone to their corners. A sad state of affairs, but reality, nevertheless. Moping around wouldn't solve the issue, and the rumbling going on in his stomach reminded him he needed to solve the problem of what his next meal would be.

A knock sounded on the door, and he looked at it hesitantly. Either Chuck had stopped by for a visit or one of the tenants had an emergency. He stifled a groan and walked over to open the door.

His brother stood on the doorstep with a takeout bag from the Sassy Spoon. *Thank You, Lord.* Michael stepped back to let him in.

"I brought dinner. Figured you hadn't eaten yet."

Michael wanted to ask what brought him by, but hadn't he just got done praying for a way to bridge the gap with his siblings? Plus, Chuck had food. "Thanks."

"Sure. I know I flaked the other day and left you with your tenant, but I was trying to be helpful. She's cute and you haven't been on a date in a while."

Michael rubbed his beard. "True." To the date, not Vivian's looks. "You do know I'm capable of finding my own dates, right?"

Chuck shrugged. "Sure, Mike. You date every day." His brother rolled his eyes, a smirk curving his mouth.

They sat on the couch while Chuck began pulling out plastic containers filled with mouthwatering burgers and fries. Michael was like one of Pavlov's dogs. His stomach grumbled with anticipation.

"Should I grab napkins?" he asked.

"Nah. Ma Spooner threw some in."

"Plates?"

Chuck smirked.

"No plates," Michael murmured.

He sat next to his brother, said grace and bit into the burger.

"I probably should have ordered you something different since you had one of those the other day."

"There's no such thing as too many hamburgers."

"Sure there is. Probably around the time you get gout."

"Medical professionals," he muttered jokingly.

They sat in silence, chewing their food. When Michael's dinner was half-finished, he broke the silence. "What brings you by?"

"Do I need a reason?" Chuck countered.

"'Course not. I was merely curious."

"Hmm. Sounded judgmental."

Sure Chuck would think that. He had a problem with anything Michael did. "How was work?" That was a safe topic, right?

"Do you really care?"

Michael counted to ten. "I do, in fact. If not, I wouldn't have asked."

Chuck eyed him warily, then nodded. "It was a long day. I think there's a virus going around in town, so steer clear of others if possible and wash your hands."

"I figured something was up. I got tasked with the

Christmas Wishes project because the Richardses got sick."

"How's that going?"

"Vivian's working on it with me. We're trying to see if we can get everyone on the list something."

Chuck let out a low whistle. "Is that possible?"

"We're trying our best. Got some of the local businesses to donate items."

"Smart. Is there anything the clinic can donate?"

Michael cocked his head to the side. "You know, I think someone on the list needs medicine."

"They're missing their meds?" Chuck frowned. "That's not good."

"No, I think they have a chronic illness and the prescription for it is costly."

"That doesn't surprise me, unfortunately. Text me what they need, and I'll talk to Doc. If he's got an in on lowering the cost or whatever, I'll let you know."

"That'd be amazing."

"It's what family is for, right?" Chuck pierced Michael with a look.

Michael readily agreed, unsure what the meaning was behind the intense expression on his brother's face. "Do we need to talk about something?"

"Nah." Chuck looked away. "We're good."

Michael heard the words, examined the neutral tone they were spoken in. Yet the hairs on the back of his neck still stood up, and he wondered if they really were okay.

Chapter Six

No matter how long she stared at the contact in her cell phone, Vivian couldn't bring herself to hit the call button. She desperately wanted to speak to her parents. To tell them how well she was doing and about her new job. How she liked answering the phone, if only to connect people with the pastor. How warmly everyone she'd met in Willow Springs treated her.

Despite the happiness she was discovering in the quaint town, her heart longed for reconciliation with her parents. *Lord God, help me, please.* She bit her lip and pressed Call, then placed the phone up to her ear.

It rang once before a recording came on the line. "The person you are dialing is unavailable at this time."

Vivian frowned. Her mother was always available. Her cell might as well be a second appendage. She tapped the edge of her phone against her chin. Was it possible her mother had blocked her number? Vivian's stomach dropped, and her eyes welled with tears.

"No," she whispered. Mom wasn't that cruel. There had to be some other reason. Maybe her phone was out of range.

Then it hit her. Vivian didn't have her old cell phone. It

had been damaged in the car crash, and she'd purchased a prepaid phone at Walmart. *Of course.* Her mother didn't answer unknown numbers. Vivian would have to text her the number and pray she responded.

She opened her messages and quickly drafted a note. A little lengthy for a text, but her mom would read it.

Mom,
I don't know what more to say that hasn't been said in my previous letters. So instead, I'll leave you with my number in case you ever want to get in touch. I'm still sober and I'm working as a church receptionist in a town called Willow Springs, between the Ozarks and Buffalo River. I love you.
Viv

Her heart pulsed steady in her ears as her finger hovered over the send button. On an exhale, she pushed it and closed the text. Now to pray that Mom would have mercy and call.

She got up, leaving her cell on the sofa in the living area. A quick glance in the refrigerator told Vivian she could have pasta, a sandwich or—she opened the freezer door—a TV dinner. She grabbed the jar of pasta sauce and the tortellini chilling in the fridge. Garlic bread would be nice with the meal, but she hadn't seen any in Michael's store.

Her phone rang, and her pulse picked up. Had her mom read the text already? She rushed from the kitchen area to the sofa and picked up the phone, frowning at the private number. Still, she swiped the green telephone icon.

"Hello?"

"Vivian, it's Ann."

Oh. Her shoulders dropped. "Hi, Ms. Ann."

"Listen. Some of the ladies from the Springs want to take you out and get to know you. Are you busy? Have you eaten?"

She stared at the pot of water. *Ugh.* She'd forgotten to turn on the stove. "I haven't."

"Great. Come on down to Starts and Stops, and I'll introduce you to everyone."

Everyone? How many ladies would be there? Still, Vivian wanted to meet new people. Settle in Willow Springs. She just wished her mom had called. "Thanks, Ms. Ann."

"My pleasure, sweetie. Should I text the address or have you seen the place?"

"Um, I'm not sure where it's at." But it wasn't like she'd get lost in Willow Springs. Wait, it was after work hours. "Could you give me a ride?"

"Oh, well, it's right next to the boutique."

Vivian knew where that was. Finding a way there would spare her the explanation of needing a ride. "Left or right of it?"

"Left if you're looking from the street."

"Thanks. See you soon."

"We can't wait."

After searching for an Uber in the area (and finding one), Vivian put her would-be dinner away, then dumped the water into the sink. She peered down at her clothes, trying to decide if she should change or not. Maybe the slacks could be exchanged for dark-wash jeans. Her lavender-colored sweater would dress up the jeans but also appear more casual.

She made the change, then grabbed her coat and purse before stepping outside and locking up the tiny house. The crisp evening air greeted her, making her skin prickle with chills despite the layers covering her arms.

She hunched forward as her steps propelled her from the back of the general store to the gravel lot in front.

A black sedan pulled up with an Uber sign in the mirror. She settled into the back thankful she could avoid the risk and embarrassment of breathing into the tube in her own car.

The device would remain on her car for six months. If she remained sober the entire time, the courts would remove it and wipe her slate clean.

Would it look suspicious if she drove to the church then walked to Starts and Stops? Or maybe it wouldn't even be a problem. After all, the sun had already set, and it was dark. Then again, Main Street had streetlights that illuminated the sidewalks and the available street parking.

Part of her wanted to tell Ms. Ann what had happened just so someone would know and the burden of keeping this a secret would be slightly relieved. The other part was far too worried about the backlash and condemnation she could possibly face.

As they entered downtown Willow Springs, all thoughts of her sobriety and past fled. Her eyes widened at the beautiful Christmas decor lighting the streets. Wreaths hung from the streetlights, and the poles had been decorated in red and white ribbon. Each business was now lit with festive bulbs and sported a decorative window display. The only thing missing was snow, and the way the weather had been acting the last few years, Vivian wouldn't be surprised if they did in fact have a white Christmas.

The Uber driver pulled up right in front of a green stone building next to the boutique, just as Ms. Ann had relayed. She thanked him and opened the back door.

Her pulse jittered as she walked up the sidewalk and

pulled the door open. Immediately the sweet scent of baked goods greeted her. Her stomach awoke in appreciation at the scent of…was that strawberry pie?

"Vivian!"

Her gaze snagged at the hand waving in the back of the restaurant. The shotgun style allowed for multiple tables in a single column. She passed the other people as she headed to the table Ms. Ann was rising from.

"You made it." Ms. Ann hugged Vivian tight.

"Thanks for inviting me," she murmured.

"Of course." They broke apart, and Ms. Ann pointed to the woman closest to Vivian. "This is Cecelia, and Yvonne is sitting next to her."

"Nice to meet you," Vivian greeted.

"You as well." Cecelia smiled. Her black pixie cut was reminiscent of Toni Braxton, as was the color of her skin.

"We saved you a seat." Yvonne, the one with a brown bob, pointed to the empty spot across from her.

Vivian could detect a slight accent that seemed to have Latin influence.

"Thanks." She squeezed behind Ms. Ann's chair and sat down.

Huh. Ms. Ann seemed to be the oldest one in the group. Vivian didn't know exactly what she'd expected from the invite, but it wasn't two other women close to her own age.

Yvonne leaned forward. "So, inquiring minds want to know why you moved to Willow Springs." She flashed a smile. "Don't worry, this is off the record."

Fear gripped its talons around her heart. "Excuse me?" She reached for the glass of water and gulped half of it down.

"Yvonne works for the town newspaper." Cecelia flashed sympathetic eyes at Vivian. "But she keeps our conversations private no matter how much a story pricks at her."

"Oh." What else was she supposed to say to that? Her skeletons should be safe in her closet, but sitting across from a reporter made Vivian feel like she had opened the closet door and turned on the light.

"No, really, why the move?"

Vivian wasn't sure if Yvonne was pushy or merely curious. So she'd take her questions at face value. "I needed a change. Something simpler and more authentic." Did that make sense?

Judging from three smiles shining back at her, it held a commonality they could all understand. Vivian slowly relaxed her shoulders as they moved away from her past and into how she felt about living in Willow Springs.

Yet somehow, Vivian couldn't help thinking that dodging one inquiry into her background didn't mean it would never come up again.

Michael glanced at the passenger seat of his truck. Vivian sat there quietly as he drove down the winding road from the general store into town. They were headed to visit the Diaz family, who lived a few blocks away from Main Street. Michael had printed out some vouchers for groceries, while Vivian had put together a gift basket of basic necessities. They'd decided to do another basket later for Christmas dinner fixings.

"Do you really want to wait for someone to notice the basket before we leave?" His voice interrupted the stillness of the cab.

"I do. What if someone tries to steal it?"

"In Willow Springs? Besides, we could be waiting until dark." He glanced at her just in time for her to throw a look of irritation his way. "What?"

"I heard that Maria gets home around three after picking up her kids from school. Since it's two thirty now, we have time to drop the basket on the porch and hide in a spot she can't see us to ensure the gift is safe."

He stuffed down his irritation. It would be nice to ensure the Diaz family got their Christmas wish. "Fine."

"Great. I hope they don't feel like this is charity."

He hadn't thought of that and was a little surprised Vivian had. Alicia never donated to charity or offered to lend anyone a hand. Maybe that should have been the first flag something was off with her.

Was she doing well in his old job of marketing, or had someone figured out he was actually the brains behind her ideas? Then again, what did he care? He'd settled back into Willow Springs and didn't miss anything about the hustle and bustle of his old job, Well, okay, maybe heading their annual charity drives.

"How are you liking Willow Springs?" he asked.

Michael didn't know much about Vivian—and preferred it that way—but he didn't want to be rude. Since it was just the two of them in the car, with no mediator to ensure the conversation carried on, he had to bridge the silence.

"It's really peaceful here. Ms. Ann invited me to Starts and Stops last night, and I met two other women. That was nice."

"Oh, man. I love that place. Did you have their famous strawberry pie?" His mouth watered simply thinking about it.

"I did. It was amazing."

"Next time try one of their puddings. Puts those cups Pop used to include in our lunch bag to shame."

Vivian's laugh was airy. "All right. I'll have to remember that."

Silence descended once more. When Michael turned onto the street and spotted the Diaz family's small bungalow, relief pooled in his stomach. No more awkward small talk. He put the gear in Park and unbuckled.

"Which house is it?" Vivian asked.

"That yellow one."

"How adorable."

He wasn't sure what made a house adorable, but he didn't want to engage by asking the question. Being around Vivian was a constant act of biting his tongue. Something about her made him want to peel back the layers and get to know her, despite the very real desire to *not* know her and just get through her six-month stay unscathed. *What if she renews her lease?*

He batted the question away. "You ready to do this?"

"Yes."

They got out of the truck, Vivian reaching in the back for the basket. He glanced around the neighborhood, but all was quiet. Probably due to the cold temperatures that had most people wanting to stay indoors versus outside. They hurried to the home, and Vivian placed the basket on the welcome mat.

She'd filled it with items to make a charcuterie board, including the wooden board and a variety of cheeses, meats, fruits and crackers. The coupon booklet dangled from a ribbon attached to the wicker handle.

"You did a good job on the basket."

"Thanks. It was fun. I looked on Pinterest for some ideas."

Was that another social media app? He couldn't keep up with all of them. "I would have just asked one of my sisters."

"Do they ever come to visit?" Vivian asked as they headed back to his truck.

"It's been a while."

"Do you ever visit them?"

He froze, his hand hovering on the door handle. "I haven't," he said slowly.

Suddenly he didn't feel like the best big brother. How many times had he complained that they didn't answer his calls or come back home? When had he ever thought of going out to visit them? Not that running a store and rental property made getting away easy, but still.

Michael cleared his throat. "What about you? How often do you see your family?"

Vivian shifted in her seat and stared out her window. "I don't."

He searched for some words of comfort—anything to ease the tension that had filled the cab and made him want to lower the window to help it escape. "I'm sorry."

"So am I, but it is what it is."

"Doesn't make it feel any better."

She huffed. "That's the truth."

So, they both had family issues. The commonality shouldn't chip at the shield around him, but he felt a piece crumble regardless. Michael glanced over at the quiet woman next to him. The one who had his senses screaming danger but his mind cataloging the kindness and gentle way with which she approached life.

"Want to go to Mason's tree farm after someone gets the basket? I need a tree for the store."

"Okay," she said quietly.

"If you'd rather not, you can say no. I just thought it might lift our spirits." He'd rather count his blessings than wonder where it all went wrong with his life.

"No. I didn't mean anything negative by not enthusiastically agreeing. It sounds like fun."

"We'll make sure it is."

Ten minutes later, Maria Diaz came home and picked up their gift. They high-fived each other, then Michael headed toward the outskirts of Willow Springs, where the tree farm resided. They kept the conversation light on the way to Mason's land.

Soon, rows and rows of white pine and Virginia pine trees came into view, sprawled across the field. The parking lot wasn't brimming with cars, but the space wasn't empty, either.

"I've never been to a tree farm," Vivian admitted as they trudged across the gravel to the entrance.

"Never ever?"

She shook her head. "Nope. My mom always had an artificial tree because Dad has allergies."

"We always got our trees from here. We would take turns sawing the trunk until it fell. Then Pop would haul it back home."

"And y'all always lived above the store?"

"Yep. It has three bedrooms. One for our parents, one for Chuck and me, and the other for the girls."

"Sounds cozy and homey."

"Our parents made it that way." Now he felt the responsibility to do the same, even if all his siblings couldn't come home for Christmas. Pippen hadn't returned his calls to let him know if she would be coming. But three out of four was nothing to sneeze at.

"Our house was too much for a family of three. I often envied people who had a sibling or two to ease the loneliness."

"Ironic that most people with siblings would like a moment or two of peace."

"What we don't have is always more attractive than what we do."

Michael made a noise of agreement. He'd spent too

many years chasing what others had when he'd worked in the corporate world. Since he'd moved back to Willow Springs, all that stress had slowly melted away. Of course, he had new stressors, but even that didn't make him want to return to his previous life.

"So how do we do this?" Vivian asked. "Just find a tree and chop it down? We don't have a saw."

He chuckled. "No, they have them. We can either chop one down ourselves or pick from the precut lot." He pointed to the right.

Vivian glanced right, then left, then up at him. "Let's do it your way. I wouldn't mind chopping down a tree."

"Let's go."

Her cheeks bunched with giddiness, and he suppressed laughter. Michael didn't want her to think he was making fun of her. Her excitement was simply contagious. They checked out a saw from the stand, then walked down row after row searching for the perfect tree.

Vivian made a cry of happiness. "This is it." She gestured to the one she'd stopped by. "It'll be perfect for the store." Then she shifted to the one next to it. "And this one for your home."

He hadn't planned on getting two trees, but she had a point. He couldn't just decorate the store. His pop wouldn't have.

"Two trees, huh?"

She nodded.

"All right, Ms. Dupre. Let's get to sawing."

Chapter Seven

Vivian hadn't stopped smiling yet. She stretched her arm up and hung a black ornament near the top of the tree. When Michael had first opened the box of decorations, she'd been shocked to see some of the ornaments were black. Then he explained they were the Hogs' color. Since she'd gone to the University of Arkansas, she immediately understood the concept of a tree decorated to represent the Razorbacks, affectionately known as the Hogs.

She and Michael each grabbed ornaments—the other colors were red and white—and put them on the tree. Michael had turned on a John Legend Christmas CD for them to listen to while they decorated. He'd also invited his brother, Chuck, to the decorating party. By the time Chuck arrived with dinner, they should have the tree in the store finished and could work on the one Michael had dragged to the apartment upstairs.

"Your family always decorates the tree in here Razorback style?"

"Every year," Michael stated. "What about you? Any traditions in your family?"

Her face heated. "Well, uh, my mom always went all

out, but she never let me or Dad help. Once I was old enough to have my own place, I stuck to a tabletop tree."

"Then this is your first official tree-decorating experience?" He paused, holding a white ornament near a lower branch.

Vivian swallowed. "Maybe?"

Michael chuckled. "I'm glad I took you to the farm and have music playing, then. It's all part of the ambience."

"Is that right?"

"Yes, ma'am." He grabbed a candy cane. "As are the candy canes."

"What? We eat them while we work?"

"No. We hang them on the tree. Sometimes kids come in with their parents, and they take a peppermint as a treat. When the tree gets low, I refill it."

"That's kind of amazing, but what about parents—don't they deserve a treat?"

Michael threw his head back and let out a belly laugh. Vivian stared, transfixed, wondering why the sight froze her and the sound made her listen for every nuance of the moment. He shook his head, his laughter subsiding.

"I'll have to remember to let an adult grab one the next time someone asks."

She faked a gasp. "I can't believe you've been denying them all these years. They probably buy their candy canes somewhere else, thinking you're a Scrooge."

"Nah." He chuckled. "It's kind of like the jar of candy on Ms. Ann's desk—kids go by after church or Sunday school to ask for a piece, and every adult remembers when they were in their shoes."

"Well, now I feel terrible for taking one on my first day." She tilted her head. "Does that mean I'll have to carry out the tradition when she's no longer here?"

"You bet. The kids might start crying if they see that jar missing."

A knock sounded, and Vivian peeked out the front window.

"Chuck made it." Michael moved through the closed general store and opened the door. "Hey, brother."

"It's cold out there." Chuck shivered and passed the takeout bag to Michael. "Please tell me you have the heat blazing."

"Thin blood."

"Nah, son. It's freezing."

Vivian shook her head at their antics as they continued to rib each other.

"Let's head upstairs," Michael suggested.

"Y'all finished the Hogs tree?"

"Just about." Vivian stepped back, glancing up at the tall pine. Michael had already placed the star, which was great, because her short reach wouldn't have made it to the top.

"I can add the candy canes and meet you up there," Vivian offered. That would give the brothers time to settle and get any awkwardness out of the way. She hoped.

"Really?" Michael asked.

"Thanks, Vivian." Chuck sent her a charming smile, blowing into his cupped hands.

"Sure, go get warm."

"You don't have to tell me twice." He waved and headed for the staircase in the back.

The one Michael had showed her earlier when curiosity had prompted her to ask how he went upstairs. She had to admit, the thought of going inside his home unnerved her a little. It seemed something a girlfriend would do, and they were so not even near that realm of a relationship. But parts of her had wondered, *what if?*

What if she'd met Michael before? Before loneliness had her reaching for a bottle. Before she'd been unable to say no to having one more drink, let alone the amount she'd consumed on that fateful night.

What would he think if he knew she'd been in county lockup a couple of weeks before? Would he be disgusted or understand the person he saw today was not the person of yesterday? She blew out a breath and placed the last candy cane on a bough.

Even she had trouble believing she was a new creation at times. Like yesterday, when she'd been at Starts and Stops with the other ladies. Spotting dessert cocktails on the menu, Vivian had grown warm worrying that she would have a relapse, but she'd resisted the urge. The relief that had flooded her had been instant. All she could do was thank the Lord for helping her avoid the precarious situation. She stared at the star on top of the tree, imagining the wise men who had looked toward one as a compass to find Christ.

Lord, thank You for being my compass. Thank You for saving me.

She couldn't thank Him enough for how He'd changed her. All she could hope was the change remained everlasting. She didn't want to slip up, and her sponsor had warned Vivian of the potential. Alcoholism was a disease, and sobriety wasn't a cure. But she'd worked the steps toward recovery and a new way of life. Her faith had been the catalyst for radical change and healing. Moving to Willow Springs was simply the next step in her recovery process. She no longer wanted to chase after accolades in a high-paying job—she simply wanted to live out the will of God for her life.

Being part of the Christmas Wishes ministry was helping her see the good in the world and that she could be part of that. Never before had she cared to help others, so enjoying that change in herself was something to glorify God for.

She slid her hands inside her hoodie pocket and headed for the back of the store. Hopefully the guys had had enough time to work out the lingering discomfort she spied whenever they were in the same room. She climbed the steps, quietly so as to not disturb them. And to steady her nerves before she entered Michael's home.

"Y'all looked kind of cozy downstairs," Chuck stated, spreading the food out on the dining room table.

Michael rolled his eyes as he reached for plates, then grabbed some silverware from the drawer. "Because we were hanging ornaments?"

"Nah, the whole atmosphere. Music playing—"

"Christmas music."

"Lights dimmed—"

"To see the Christmas tree better."

"And talking quietly."

"Because we were within two feet of each other and didn't need to shout." Michael set the stack of dishes on the table. "She's my tenant."

Chuck raised an eyebrow. "If that's what you want to claim."

"Do you just want to see me married with a bunch of kids so you can call yourself Uncle Chuck?"

"I just want you to have some kind of happiness. Ever since Pop died, you've been a hermit up on this hill, giving your all to this land."

"It was Pop's place! How could I turn my back on it?" Michael threw his hands out to his side, anger rising at Chuck's needling.

"Like me?" Chuck murmured.

"I never said that."

"But maybe you silently judged."

Michael huffed, rubbing the back of his neck. "You have a job. You're a nurse. You've always taken care of others." It was true. Growing up, Chuck had been the one playing doctor when the rest of them got sick.

Except he didn't go to med school but nursing school. So maybe he judged that, but never keeping his career instead of helping out at the house. *Right?*

"Yeah, but sometimes I get the feeling you're disappointed I don't do more to help around here."

Maybe a little. Michael was beginning to think this thing bugging Chuck was bigger than he fathomed. "Working the store and the rentals *has* been a lot, but I never expected you to help, since you have a full-time job. And not just a job, but a career." Michael blew out a breath. "Since Pop was killed by that drunk driver—"

A gasp halted his speech, and he whirled around to find Vivian standing in the entryway, all color leached from her face.

He winced. People didn't know what to say to someone who had lost a loved one. Worse, when their life was shortened because they'd been murdered. And vehicular homicide was no different from any other form of homicide, except the choice of weapon was a vehicle.

"A drunk driver killed your dad?" Vivian wrung her hands.

Michael walked forward before he was even conscious of the movement. It wasn't until he reached for her hands that he was aware he'd crossed the room. "Hey, it's okay." Well, not really, but wasn't that what you said to help another person? "The doctor said he died instantly."

Tears welled in Vivian's dark brown eyes and spilled over. "I'm so sorry. I can't… I just… I'm so sorry."

"Don't cry," he pleaded while guiding her to the sofa.

She reacted as if she'd received a shock, and he knew just how that felt. Recalled that tight feeling in his chest, like he couldn't get a proper breath, and his feet feeling like they had been encased in wet cement. The fog took days to clear, and once it had, the grief took its place. Had she lost a loved one in the same way?

"I didn't mean to upset you."

Vivian's brow furrowed. "*Your* father died, not mine. You didn't upset me. I guess I didn't realize how he died..." Her voice trailed off.

Michael nodded. "It was a shock to all of us."

"Unfortunately," Chuck added. He came to sit on the coffee table in front of Vivian. "How you feeling? Can I check your pulse?"

Vivian startled, and a strangled laugh escaped her lips. "I'm not in shock. At least, not medically."

"You sure?" Chuck asked.

"Positive." She ran a hand down her ponytail. "Um, maybe I should just head to my place and let you decorate the tree together. After all, y'all are family."

And she was not. Michael heard the words as clear as day. He hadn't meant to make her uncomfortable and certainly didn't want her leaving after such a bombshell. "I'd like your company, if you want to stay. But if not, we understand." He discreetly nudged his brother.

"Definitely. Whatever works for you, Vivian."

She bit her lip. "I wouldn't mind decorating another tree."

"Great." Chuck clapped his hands together. "Because I'm terrific at directing traffic."

Vivian chuckled, and relief seeped into Michael's shoulders. He hadn't even realized they'd been held tightly near his ears. He rolled his neck, then got up and headed to the table.

"We should eat first," he called to them.

"Yes, please." Chuck whispered close to him, "Maybe keep the topic light so the lady won't cry again."

"My bad." Michael spoke low enough for only Chuck to hear.

"Sure, sure."

"Thanks for dinner, Chuck." Vivian smiled.

"My pleasure. Especially since you helped Michael get the trees. It's a thank-you."

"Then you're welcome."

Dinner was a lot more low-key compared to how the four Wood siblings grew up. Mom and Pop would always corral them to the dining table after making them wash their hands. Then they would say grace, each child getting a chance to deliver the prayer—typically ending in a clamor for attention from their parents while stuffing their faces.

Mom had always reminded them to use their manners, while Pop would grin cagily and egg them on. Now it was Michael, Chuck and Vivian talking at a normal volume about the Christmas pageant coming up at church.

"They do this every year?" Vivian asked.

"Yes, ma'am. The kids love to be picked for a chance to be in the play, and the parents dab their eyes while the children recite the memorized lines." Michael winked at Chuck, remembering the year he played a lamb.

"Who's in charge?" she asked.

"The Whites. They run the children's ministry." Chuck paused. "Has Ms. Ann introduced you to everyone?"

"If they've come into the office. I did see some faces at the last service, but they haven't stuck in my head yet."

"You'll remember everyone's names sooner or later,"

Michael interjected. "Willow Springs is small, and you'll run into someone repeatedly before the week's out."

She chuckled. "I ran into Ma Spooner at the post office."

"See what I mean?"

Once they finished their food, Chuck grabbed the decorations from the hall closet as Michael made sure the tree stood centered before the window overlooking the front parking lot.

As they began outfitting the pine with ornaments, Michael spared a glance at Vivian. Gone were the tears and heartbroken demeanor. Her frown had literally been turned upside down. The thought made him think of his mom.

Lord God, please get my brother and sisters home for Christmas. Help us to be close again. The dream team had fractured with the loss of their parents, but he wouldn't lose hope they could be hewn together once more. If Michael could have any prayer answered by Christmastime, that would be it. To heal the rift between them all and restore them as a unit.

Chapter Eight

The black liquid in Vivian's coffee mug seemed endless, much like the barrage of questions that she had played over and over in her mind since she'd first heard Michael say his father had been killed by a drunk driver. Who? What? When? Where? Why?

Unfortunately, she could answer the why. It was all too easy to believe that you were in full control despite the number of drinks you'd consumed. After all, a person's body adjusted to consumption the longer they imbibed. That had been one of the excuses Vivian had used. Either that, or she'd told herself all her friends were more drunk than she, so at least she could get herself safely home versus one of them being behind the wheel.

After the first time she'd driven herself home, barely missing her mailbox, she'd promised not to drive intoxicated again. But it had taken slamming into the back of an empty police car—her first official offense—for her problem with alcohol to really sink in. She'd had to hear the clank of the jail cell locking and view her new reality behind bars before she admitted she needed help.

Inmates had no choice but to dry out in county jail. Still, there were those who tried to find ways to sneak in contraband. Vivian had steered clear and attended the AA meetings instead. It wasn't until she talked to Kate, the outsider who led the meetings and later became her sponsor, that Vivian began to examine the root causes of her alcoholism. When Kate suggested church, Vivian had gone just to get out of the small space with her noisy cellmate.

A month into her sentence, something like a switch lit in her head and Vivian began to truly listen to the sermons. To examine herself and the lackadaisical attitude she'd exhibited up until then. She'd been excited to make the correlation between feeling unloved growing up and trying to collect accolades as if they could fill up the dry well inside her. Being an only child of two high-achieving adults who were always busy left her lonely. When she made the decision to accept Christ as her savior, peace flooded her heart.

But now, that peace was horribly absent, and she could only focus on what Michael had lost. How could she ever tell him why she'd been sent to jail? Would he ask her to move out? Would he ask Ms. Ann to find someone else to do the Christmas Wishes program with him?

She sniffled, lowering the coffee mug to the table. She wasn't doing anything but soaking in the warmth, as she just couldn't seem to rid the chill from her bones. Not after the news of Michael's father's death. But the thought of losing all she was building in Willow Springs crowded in.

Working on the Christmas Wishes program reminded her of why she'd turned her life around—to help people feel loved and give them a spark of hope when life seemed intent on snuffing it out. She still remembered the delight she'd felt when she'd seen Maria Diaz spot the basket on her doorstep. Relief had flooded the woman's facial features, and her burden had seemed a little lighter.

But if Vivian's past were to come to light…

She shook her head and rose to her feet. There was nothing to gain from sitting there moping about her past. She was alive and needed to be thankful for that much. Slamming into the police cruiser could have gone an entirely different direction. She was just glad the car had been empty. The fact hadn't stopped her from going to County, but at least she didn't have vehicular homicide or manslaughter on her conscience.

Her phone chimed with an alert, and she picked it up. She unlocked the phone and blinked at the number one by her text icon. Stacey will be working at the bookstore this morning. Want to go by and hand her the plane ticket?

Vivian gasped, excitement filtering through her. She couldn't wait to see the look on Stacey's face when they presented her with the airfare voucher to see her family. Someone would be surrounded by loved ones this Christmas, that Vivian was sure of. Yes!

Meet you in 10?

She sent a thumbs-up emoji and proceeded to clean up her morning mess. Ten minutes later, she found herself riding in the passenger side of Michael's truck.

"How's your morning going?" she asked.

Michael groaned.

"That well?"

His lips tilted enough to erase the frown and edge toward a smile.

"Want to talk about it?"

He glanced at her, then back at the road. "Are you sure you want to hear about it?"

Wasn't listening to another's problems better than weeding through her own? "Yes. Let's hear it." She made a hand motion like *bring it on* and smiled when Michael chuckled softly.

She'd ignore the part where his laughter made her want an alternate reality in which she'd met him before her life had self-destructed.

"We got some new tenants in. Apparently, they like to party."

"Really?" Vivian frowned. She hadn't heard any noises. "What kind of party?"

"The excessive drinking variety. They left the trash area, well…*trashed.* Fortunately, I only caught some raccoons and not an animal that would have us all wishing we were safe in our homes."

Her nose wrinkled, imagining the scene. It all hit too close to home. "Was it a lot to clean up?"

"Yes, which meant I couldn't open the store on time."

"Why don't you hire cleaning help?"

"Can't afford to. Not unless I can get the tiny homes rented at full capacity."

"By that time, you may be stretched to the max."

"I feel the pull already."

Vivian wanted to lay her hand on his arm and offer a word of comfort. That seemed way too personal, so she settled for a sympathetic tone. "I'm so sorry."

"Yeah. The Markinsons stopped by and weren't too thrilled I opened an hour late. They found me cleaning up outside and informed me they'd be back in an hour or else."

"Or else what? They'd make the drive to Walmart?" *How rude!* Why hadn't they offered to lend a hand? Vivian would have if she'd known.

"Nah, they're an elderly couple. They don't like driving outside Willow Springs. Mr. Markinson probably should have his driver's license revoked."

"Too bad someone couldn't pick up his groceries for him or do errands like that for the elderly in the community."

"That's a pretty great idea. I'll have to keep that in mind the next time someone says they want to help around town."

"So will I, then." She added a soft smile to the end of the words. Lending Michael a listening ear might not have relieved his stress completely, but the lines between his brows were smoothing out.

"Thanks for listening."

"Of course. Anytime." She cleared her throat. Why had she tacked on that last part? Not that he would necessarily take her up on her offer. So maybe it was fine she'd extended it.

"Thanks."

Vivian stared out the window, trying to pull a conversation starter or any topic to mind instead of weighing the silence between them, but her brain was blank.

Michael exhaled, happy that his shoulders felt less pressure and the worry giving him a tension headache had alleviated some. Whether that was because he was able to complain about the short-term tenants or due to the attentiveness that Vivian bestowed upon him while he vented, he felt thankful. He'd never imagined when they first met that she would have such a way about her that settled some of his inner turmoil. Granted, she also seemed to stir up some of his emotions as well.

The kind that had Chuck's words repeating in his head, reminding him just how long it had been since he'd dated. Not that he'd been a serial dater before. But after leaving a serious relationship and then keeping away from the entire female populace, noticing one registered on the Richter scale.

Vivian seemed to be genuinely kind, as if she had no ulterior motive. Part of him wanted to trust what his head believed, but another nitpicked every single thought for consistency. Not to mention to keep him from making such a foolish mistake again. No way he would fall for a pretty woman's tricks a second time.

"How'd you know Stacey works at the bookstore?" Vivian asked in the still quiet.

"Oh, I ran into Ms. Ann, who wanted an update on the project. I asked about a few people on the list I was unsure of as far as where they worked or lived. She filled me in, and that's how I found out Stacey works at Buy the Book."

He glanced at Vivian in time to see her smile. "I love the names here. They're so apt for each trade."

"You don't think they're a little on the nose?"

She chuckled. "Yes, but that's what makes it fun. Like Simplicity Rentals."

"Well, I did try and be less obvious."

"Nothing simpler than a two-hundred-square-foot home."

"Is that a bad thing? I really thought this was a great idea when I first started. Now I have my doubts." Did he ever. They kept him up at night sometimes.

Like, could he continue making the payments on the reverse mortgage Pop had taken out while making rental repairs and buying produce and other wares to stock the store? What happened if he added more homes to the lot? Would it sink him further into debt or be the pull he needed to bring him into the black?

"Did you pray about your decision before doing it?" Vivian asked.

Michael arched an eyebrow. "Uh…maybe?"

"Maybe you acknowledge that you forged ahead without prayer and ask God for guidance now?"

"Hmm." He would like to think he was a better man than the thoughts in his head portrayed him. Because her suggestion—while obviously from a good heart—needled and brought the tension seeping back in.

Vivian was a new Christian. She'd said so herself. So what made her think she could counsel him on how to live his life? Well, okay, he could grudgingly admit he probably should have prayed over the situation instead of looking at the debt Pop left him and jumping right to fix-it mode. Only at this moment, he didn't want to give any validity to her comment.

"I'm sorry," she murmured. "Maybe I shouldn't have said anything. I'm new to this whole thing. That just seemed like the logical first step."

Oh, man. Pile on the guilt while she was at it. Then again, his guilt wasn't her fault, but his. Maybe he wouldn't feel like jumping out of a moving vehicle if he'd done the right thing in the beginning.

He sighed. "Nothing to be sorry over. Just hit a little close to home, you know?" He spared her a glance and caught her nodding.

"Definitely. Like you wish you could turn back time for a do-over, or at least erase some of the consequences as easily as God says you're forgiven."

Michael sighed. Wouldn't that be nice. "Why are we so hard on ourselves?"

"We're human, and we operate in that capacity."

"What do you mean?"

"Well..." She paused.

He waited, hoping that whatever she shared would make sense and give him some kind of direction.

"I mean, we're not God and we'll never be, so we can't see the things He does or how a situation will turn out. We only have the view in front of us and the guidance left to us from the Bible. How we operate in life depends on how much we've soaked in from our time with Him and the Word. How much we trust what's in front of us versus what He says."

Huh. That was actually pretty insightful. Come to think of it, outside church, when was the last time he'd cracked open his Bible?

Conviction rolled through him, and it was all he could do to keep driving instead of pulling over and falling to his knees to ask for forgiveness. "You might be new at this, but I feel like you've been blessed with a heap of wisdom and discernment."

"Really?"

The uncertainty and vulnerability in her voice almost gutted him. "Really. Whatever you're doing, keep doing it."

"I'm only trying to keep from going back to my old self. I don't want to be that woman anymore, and I certainly don't want to disappoint the Lord. He's done so much for me."

"I can understand that. Make sure you don't fall into the trap of good works, though."

"What do you mean?"

"Thinking that if you volunteer more or give more or whatever *more* will gain you favor from the Lord. His forgiveness is free the moment you ask for it. If you want to do good, do so because He's guiding you to a new path.

Not because you think He'll think better of you. He loves you just the way you are. Scars, sins and all."

"Thanks for that."

"Anytime." Now if he could remember that same bit of advice for himself, maybe he'd be in better shape.

Chapter Nine

Vivian blinked as she stared at the man on her doorstep. "Bradley. What are you doing here?"

Her parole officer smirked. "Wellness check."

"Oh." She stepped back as her face heated with shame. What would she do if Michael saw Bradley at her home? Would she have to explain who he was? Not that it mattered. It's not like they were dating. She didn't owe him an explanation.

Stop making a mountain out of a molehill. Breathe.

She drew in a lungful of air and slowly blew it out.

"You hiding anything I need to be aware of? Will I get poked with a needle?" He stood just inside the door, eyeing her with suspicion.

"Alcohol was my poison, not drugs."

His glared at her.

Okay, obviously her anxiousness was making her too snarky. "I apologize. It was a horrible attempt at a joke."

"I'll say. You know people often quit one vice and jump to another."

She held up the sixty-six-book tome. "Hence the Bible."

"So, you're sticking to this Christianity stuff?" His gaze pierced her with coal-black eyes.

"It's the truth."

"Humph." Bradley walked through the tiny home, opening drawers here and there.

Probably searching for forbidden paraphernalia. Vivian had nothing to worry about, though. She'd promised to follow God's will for her life, and that meant no alcohol or anything else that would violate her parole or jeopardize her chance to strike the past incarceration from her legal record.

"How's work going for ya?" Bradley asked in his gruff voice, his fingers flipping through her Bible.

"I like it. The people are nice."

"Yeah, well, church folk gotta be better than criminals. If not, what's the point of this?"

"Considering I'm not church folk, I'd say the point is to heal us from the scars of our mistakes and grant us a second chance." She resisted the urge to arch an eyebrow and give him a pointed expression.

Because, *hello*, that's exactly what she was doing. Though some would label her a recovering alcoholic, she chose to adhere to the label of a believer and let that be her identity from now on. Everything else was just the world trying to peg her into a square hole she refused to fit in.

"Hmm," he grunted and placed the Bible back on her end table, then took a few steps to the kitchen.

He repeated the process of examining every nook and cranny, searching for... Well, nothing. Bradley wouldn't find anything, because there wasn't anything to find.

"This place looks clean."

"It is. The owner is immaculate with the rentals. He leaves us long-term renters to look after ourselves, though, so I do the cleaning on my day off." She swallowed. Why had she offered that information? It's not like he asked for it.

"If I go talk to your employer, he'll have nothing but good things to say?"

Ms. Ann or the pastor? She gulped. "Yes. I'm on time. I do what's required and more." She licked her lips. "In fact, I'm working on the Christmas Wishes project with the owner here."

"What's that?" Bradley walked a few steps to the bathroom area.

Vivian pulled at her fingers as she told him the church's mission and how she and Michael were bringing it to fruition.

"So y'all are going around playing Good Samaritan?"

Huh. She hadn't thought of it like that. "Essentially."

"Maybe you really have changed."

Despite the skepticism coating every single word, Vivian felt lighter with his proclamation. If someone like her parole officer could see a change, then that had to mean she was on the right path.

"I have, Bradley. I promise."

"I'll be honest, Vivian. I didn't care if you changed or not when I first met you. All I wanted to do was ensure you got to where you could make use of a second chance. So many inmates come out of jail or prison and fall right back into the same trap that put them there in the first place." He paused, rubbing the bald spot at his crown. "Seeing this place, hearing about your work, I really do hope it sticks. I'd actually hate to see you go back."

"I have *no* intention of stepping foot back in that place." Goose bumps pebbled her arms. "No intention," she reiterated as she rubbed her arms. It was almost like a hug to reassure herself of how far she'd come and the promise to God she made.

She would devote herself entirely to Him. She would deny herself every day if it meant that Jesus's work hadn't been in vain.

"All right then." He spread his hands up, then dropped them, taking the gloves off. "I'll see you next time, Vivian Dupre."

"Okay." She moved toward the door, opening it wide and breathing in the crisp air.

Bradley dipped his head then walked out.

Her breath flew out like a deflated balloon. She sank against the doorstep, surprised to feel tears prick the corners of her eyes. Why was she so surprised by the unexpected visit? Wellness checks were par for the course.

She racked her brain, searching for the source of the embarrassment flooding her. Maybe seeing him in Willow Springs, a place she'd equated to a new start, was enough to remind her of why she needed a second chance to begin with. Upon her release, Bradley had informed her he could pop up at any time, but she'd thought the distance from Little Rock to Willow Springs—a three-hour drive—would deter him.

"Vivian?"

She straightened, turning at the sound of her name. Michael stomped across the yard, a look of concern on his face.

"What's wrong?" she asked.

"What's wrong with *me*? What's wrong with *you*?" He made a circle around his face. "You're all pale and look uneasy."

He could tell all that? "I needed some fresh air."

"In thirty-degree weather? You know they're saying a snowstorm might turn us into a scene out of *Jack Frost*."

She shivered. "That would be amazing. I can't remember the last time we got snow."

"Weather has changed a lot in the last few years. Who knows? This may be our new normal."

Vivian wrinkled her nose. "No, thanks. It's beautiful, but I don't want a yearly reoccurrence."

Michael leaned against the doorjamb, and she froze at how much closer he was now. "Want to gift another person on the list?"

"Okay." She nodded, then stood to put distance between them.

Michael was a good man. He didn't need her baggage. *Remember, a year with no relationships.* She had to reiterate the words her sponsor had advised. Jumping into a relationship so early into her recovery wasn't a good idea.

Even if she had religion. Kate's words, not hers.

"Who's up this time?"

She could still remember the joy on Stacey's face when they handed her the plane voucher yesterday. The hug she'd blessed Vivian with had spoken louder than the thanks she'd given them. The tight squeeze declared relief, happiness, gratitude and realization of hope. Vivian had been so grateful to be part of spreading cheer in Willow Springs.

She actually couldn't imagine living anywhere else and was thankful that God had brought her to this isolated town. Though, since it wasn't near Bentonville, some might not even consider it part of northwest Arkansas, with its close proximity to the Ozarks. But northwestern Arkansas went further than the small corner of the map.

"Carter."

Vivian gasped. Carter was legally blind and had been nominated to receive a seeing-eye dog. "Stop. You got him a dog?"

Michael's gaze twinkled at the incredulous look that

surely covered her face. He made a motion for her to follow, so she grabbed a coat and locked her place. She'd trust that he would clear things up soon.

The moment he opened the door to the general store, a dog barked. Vivian huffed behind him, and he hid a smile. She'd asked him follow-up questions, but he'd told her to wait. After another round of questions, she finally did just that.

"Who is this gorgeous guy?" Vivian fell to her knees, rubbing her hands along the black Lab's coat.

"That's Samson," Michael stated. He pointed to Samson's handler. "And that's Beth. She came with Samson." He winced. "I mean, she's his handler until he can be with Carter permanently."

Lines creased around Vivian's mouth as she continued to croon to the dog. "What do you mean?"

"We got Carter accepted into the Arkansas guide dog school. Beth will be his and Samson's trainer."

Carter had been in Willow Springs a lot longer than Michael had been alive. The old man lived on the outskirts of town near the Buffalo River. His cabin looked like it was on its last legs, but Carter insisted he didn't need any help.

But someone had disagreed and requested a seeing-eye dog for Carter. His eyesight had declined over the years thanks to an eye disease. Since he was now legally blind, he qualified for a guide dog. His daughter-in-law thought a dog would give Carter the independence he wanted to hold on to. Plus, Michael had tasked some able men to help fix up Carter's home. His daughter-in-law was hopeful he would be amiable to the dog to avoid moving to a nursing home or in with his son's family.

"Carter's going to love Samson. Isn't that right, boy?"

Samson's tongue lolled out, and Michael stifled a laugh. If he didn't know any better, he'd believe the dog knew every single word Vivian uttered. Samson seemed to sit up straighter and preen under her attention.

"Beth will follow us over to Carter's place."

"Great. Let's go." Vivian stood, and Samson moved to his handler's side.

Michael led the way out of the store, ensuring the sign still said Closed. He couldn't wait to see the look on Carter's face when they showed up with the Labrador. Would he be grateful or annoyed by his family's interference? Michael prayed he would enjoy Samson's company.

As he left the lot, he glanced at Vivian. "Starts and Stops is having a gingerbread house–making contest Friday. You going?"

"I hadn't heard. But Cecelia and Yvonne invited me out Friday. Maybe I'll suggest we go to that. What about you? Do you go? Does Chuck?"

"We used to go every year as a family. It would be nice to do so again. Maybe I'll text Chuck and ask." Give himself a reason to reach out to his brother and do something fun.

"What about your sisters?"

"They don't live nearby."

"Maybe not, but perhaps they'd be willing to drive here if they knew how much it meant to you."

Had he said that? Implied it? Of course it meant a lot to him, but he hadn't realized that Vivian picked up on his feelings so well. He rubbed the back of his neck, thinking about the distance from Fayetteville to here. It was only an hour and a half. Surely they could come by, go to the gingerbread contest and stay the night in their old rooms. They'd be able to drive back home over the weekend.

"Maybe I'll do that."

"I think you should."

He'd pray about it. Which he'd been doing a whole lot more since Vivian had accused him of forgetting his first love—the Lord.

The rest of their ride was silent. Not out of awkwardness but more companionable silence. Plus, Michael kept churning over thoughts of his family. Soon he turned down a gravel road, the car bumping over various potholes.

"Sorry," he gritted out. "Carter needs to get this fixed."

"He probably doesn't get much company outside of family." Vivian held on to the door handle.

Finally, they rolled to a stop, and Michael blew out a breath. He stepped out of the vehicle and watched as Beth pulled in behind him. She opened the car door, and Samson hopped out.

The sound of a rickety screen door opening screeched through the air, and Michael paused. Carter held on to the door, his eyes unseeing as his head swiveled. Probably listening for sounds. "Who's there?"

"It's me, Carter. Michael Wood. From the general store."

"I know who you are. You're one of the dream team."

Michael smiled. "Yes, sir."

"Whatcha doing here?"

"I brought you a present, courtesy of Marcy."

"Ugh," he groaned. "My daughter-in-law is always trying to give me something. Who else you got with you?"

Michael grinned at Vivian. "Vivian Dupre, the new church secretary at the Springs."

"I've heard about her. Nice to meet you, ma'am."

"You, too, sir."

"Also Beth Page."

Carter stepped back. "Who's that?"

"I'd love to explain inside," Michael said.

"Come on in, then. Might as well get this over with."

They followed him into the house that was dark but surprisingly clean. *Probably Marcy's doing.* Carter gestured toward the lumpy sofa, and Michael sat down. Samson curled up at Beth's feet as she sat in an empty recliner.

"So let me guess. She nominated me for the Christmas Wishes ministry, huh?"

"She did," Michael answered.

"I want no part of it."

"Don't you want to know what it is before you say no?" Vivian asked quietly.

Carter's head swiveled toward her. "Guess so. What is it? A maid service? Marcy does just fine."

Michael restrained the chuckle working in his throat. "No, sir. A dog."

Carter's unseeing eyes blinked rapidly. "What ya mean?"

"She wanted to give you some independence back. Uh, why don't I let Beth tell you more?"

She nodded, tucking strands of her blond hair behind her ear. "Mr. Dawson, Samson here is a seeing-eye dog. He's been through a rigorous vetting process. When Mr. Wood contacted us, we forwarded our onboarding questionnaire to your daughter-in-law and son to fill out. Our company then matched Samson with you. You two will go through a training program where Samson will learn to meet your needs based off the commands you teach him. He'll be able to help you go places, retrieve stuff for you, the whole gamut."

"Well, I'll be," Carter breathed. "I ain't never thought of nothing like that."

Michael smiled with relief. "Marcy knows how much you want to do things on your own."

The old man's eyes welled with tears. "Suppose I've

been too harsh with her." He rubbed his chin dotted with unkempt hair. "My boy did marry up."

"I'm sure a thank-you will be good enough," Vivian assured.

Beth motioned for Samson to rise and brought him over to Carter. "Samson is right at your knee. But I can guide your hand if you need help petting him."

Carter stuck out his hand, and Beth guided his palm to Samson's back. The dog laid his head on Carter's knee, and a ragged sigh escaped the older man. "Thank you."

"You're welcome. Merry Christmas, Carter." Michael swallowed back some unexpected emotions.

"Merry Christmas to y'all."

Chapter Ten

"Ugh." Vivian blew out a breath.

As much as she liked the tiny home, right now she needed more space than it provided. She looked at the lump of cookie dough and the lack of counter space to roll it out so she could use the Christmas-inspired cookie cutters.

She washed her hands then picked up her cell, opening the text app. She typed up a message to Michael. *Hey, is there any possible way you'd let me use your kitchen to bake cookies?*

What kind?

She snorted. That's what he wanted to ask? *Sugar cookies. I have a bunch of cookie cutters and frosting to decorate with. I'll be giving them to my friends.*

How does the landlord fit into your friends database?

She laughed. He was funny in texts. *Well, I suppose since you're in my contacts, I'll count you as a friend.*

Perfect. You're welcome to my oven. I'm working in the store, so come on in and I'll let you upstairs.

Thanks. I really appreciate this.

Because even though it was after work, she wasn't tired at all. She'd been inspired to whip up some cookies by the kindness of others. Ms. Ann had gifted the church staff with homemade fudge, then the pastor had shared a fruit cake his wife had made. Everyone had seemed to get the memo that the holidays were for baked goods and to share with others. After finding a recipe on Pinterest, she bought the ingredients at the general store.

Vivian had been really surprised to see Michael had cookie cutters on the store shelf, but it was December, after all. Only, in the whole spirit of giving, she'd forgotten to take into consideration the size of her kitchen—her very *tiny* kitchen.

She gathered up her bowl of dough and other things she'd need, thankful for the reusable grocery bags to carry everything in, rushed out the door, and headed for the store. The wind nipped at her, stinging her cheeks and making her wish she'd grabbed her jacket as well. How could she forget that snow was in the forecast for Saturday? She rushed across the frosted ground, leaves crunching beneath her feet. She walked into the general store and sighed when heat greeted her.

"Hey, Vivian. Back so soon?" Michael smirked.

"I forgot I was working with a miniature kitchen."

"Sorry. I could've installed a butcher block for a dining table that could have worked as an island, but I didn't." He shrugged. "I'll try and remember that the next time I add more homes."

She nodded, not knowing how else to respond. He motioned for her to follow him up the back, and she gladly obliged. Her arms were getting heavy from the cumbersome items.

"Are you sure you're okay with me using the oven?"

"Sure. That's what neighbors do in Willow Springs."

"Really? I thought it was nothing but borrowing a cup of sugar or bringing baked goods to newbies."

"Someone brought you baked goods?"

"Well, at work, but I was more thinking of the someone who left me a welcome basket."

Michael's cheeks flushed. Vivian bit her lip to keep the surprise from showing on her face. Was he truly embarrassed she'd noticed such detail? "I never thanked you. So…thank you."

"Don't worry about it." He cleared his throat. "The oven works like most ovens in this part of the world, so you should be fine."

"Thanks."

"Mmm-hmm." He backed out of the house, waved, then jogged down the steps.

At least she thought he did. The sound was fast and a little heavy.

Vivian put her things down and immediately set to work preheating the oven and getting the dough rolled out. She got so caught up in cutting the shapes and laying them on the cookie sheet that she failed to notice Michael had come back until he reached for a bit of uncooked dough.

She smacked his hand on instinct. Her eyes widened. "I'm so sorry. I don't know why I did that."

But all he did was chuckle. "My mom used to do the same thing. Sorry, I can't resist snagging a little piece."

"Don't you know not to eat raw cookie dough?" Her heart slowed from racing to a mere jog.

"It tastes good."

"So true." She sighed. "But the cookies will be just as good."

"If you say so."

She laughed. "Want to help me frost them?"

"Sure." Michael pointed to the oven. "Got a batch in now?"

"Yep. It has another two minutes. We'll need to let them cool first before we frost them."

"Then when do we get to eat them?" He wore such a crestfallen expression.

Stranger than that was the way her heart flipped at the idea of giving him a cookie just to see him smile.

What is wrong with you? There was no point in allowing herself to feel something for Michael—no way he would ever fall for her in return. Not if he knew what she'd done. Why she'd sought refuge in Willow Springs. Plus, there was the fact she was only six months sober. That wasn't long enough to form the habit of not drinking. Or was it?

Besides, she didn't want to jump into a relationship and use it as a rebound vice like Bradley had speculated upon when he'd done his wellness check.

Vivian cleared her throat. "I'll let you have one unfrosted, but then you'll have to wait."

"Deal." His cheeks bunched with a grin.

She swatted away feelings that weren't allowed. The oven beeped, distracting her. Removing the cookie sheet and sliding in the second one gave her time to reorient her mind and stick Michael in the *friends only* box.

"Here." Michael placed a cooling rack on the counter.

"Thanks. I didn't even think about that."

"Mom always used them, and I never got rid of them."

"Did you ever call your sisters about the gingerbread

contest?" Vivian asked, thankful her hands had something to distract her. The motion of moving cookies to the cooling rack kept her mind from dwelling on the domestic picture they made in his house.

"I haven't. I've been thinking about it."

"Well, you're not working now, so it's the perfect time to move thought into action."

He cocked his head to the side. "Not going to cut me any slack, huh?"

"Not when I know how badly you want them there."

"It feels weird to call up and ask them." He blew out a breath.

"I'm sure it's just the worry over what they'll say that makes it feel awkward." She couldn't help but think of the distance between her and her parents. "Just extend the invitation, knowing you did your part. Let God work out the details." *And remember that for yourself, Viv. You've reached out to your folks. The ball is in their court.*

"Okay. I can do that." Michael pulled out his cell from his back pocket.

"Should I go downstairs and give you some privacy?"

"Yeah, because gingerbread houses are such scandalous conversation."

She chuckled. "Fine. I'll just keep quiet." While praying that his call was met with good reception.

His mind whirred as the phone rang in his ear. Michael kept his gaze affixed on Vivian as she moved around his kitchen as if she'd been living here all along and not in one of the tiny homes.

"Michael?" Jordan's voice greeted him, changing his focus.

He turned away, staring out into the living room so he

could concentrate on his little sister—the one only two years behind him in age. "Hey, Jay, how've you been?"

"Busy. You know how it is."

"Do I." He snorted, then paused, trying to find the right words.

"Is everything okay? You and Chuck good?"

"Yeah, we're fine. I was... I was actually calling to see if you'd have time to come down Friday for the gingerbread contest. We didn't get to do it last year..." His voice trailed off.

Last year they'd all been grieving for their parents, individually and as a unit. Then they'd gone their separate ways and stopped talking as often as they used to. Was it grief or something more?

"I know. I missed that. But, um, work's been really busy."

"I get that. I truly do." His eyeballs were going to bleed if he had to look at one more order form. "But it's been a while since we've done something as a family." He cleared his throat. "I miss y'all."

"Is Charles going? I'm assuming you asked him first."

"I asked him yesterday. No favoritism in the order I'm asking. Promise." Because texting Chuck was so much simpler than having a conversation these days.

"And he's going?"

"Yes."

"Well, I can't be the one to say no, can I?"

Michael chuckled.

"I'll be there. Still starts at seven?"

"It does." He grinned. "Can't wait to see you, Jay."

"You, too, Big Mike," she responded quietly.

"I'll let you go, then. Text me when you're on your way so I can keep a look out."

"I'm a big girl, *Michael*."

"I know, Jay. Just want you to be safe."

She sighed. "Thanks, big brother."

He hung up, tapping the cell on his chin. "One down, one to go."

But as his fingers paused over his contact list, his gaze became transfixed. Vivian looked so peaceful as she squeezed drops of food coloring into a bowl. Probably for the frosting. His mind thought of Alicia and how different they were. Did that mean what he saw with Vivian could be trusted? Was this cookie-baking version real or a front?

"Did you say something?"

Michael blinked. "Um, yes. Jordan is coming. Just need to call Pippen."

"Good!" She beamed, and something like joy warmed his heart.

He cleared his throat. "Do you bake cookies every year?"

"Nope." She looked up. "This is my first time."

"Really?" He walked back toward the counter, reached for a cookie on the cooling rack and bit into it. The treat crumbled in his mouth, heat and delicious flavor filling his senses. "This is good," he mumbled.

A relieved expression flitted through her pretty brown eyes. "Oh, good. I was a little worried, but the recipe seemed straightforward."

"Great job, especially for your first time."

"Thanks," she murmured.

He finished off the cookie, then held up his phone. It was getting too warm in here, and he needed a break from thoughts of asking her out. "Last call."

"You've got this." She smirked.

"I don't know. Pippen's the feisty one."

"Then I'll say a prayer."

"Oh, you didn't from the start?"

She laughed, and Michael couldn't help but feel pleased. Instead of investigating the whys, he pulled up Pip's number and hit the green phone icon.

"Brother! How are you?"

He arched an eyebrow. Was Pippen in trouble? She never sounded this excited for his call. "Hey, Pip. How are you?"

"Good. School's done for the semester, and I've been picking up work at the campus coffee shop."

"Awesome. Do you have plans for when you graduate? It's coming up."

"Yeah. I've got some feelers out but nothing definitive."

"Cool." He paused, trying to think of something else to say. "Cool."

"You said that already."

He forced a laugh as he ran a hand across his beard. Why was this so difficult? "Hey, so what are your plans for Christmas?"

"Why?" she asked cautiously.

"I was wondering if you'd come home for the gingerbread contest…and for Christmas."

"Is Jordan going? If so, I might be able to catch a ride with her."

"Yes."

"Is she leaving this Friday?"

"I didn't ask, but I would assume so. She said work was busy."

"Then after we get off the phone, I'll call and see if I can ride down with her. Thanks for asking, big brother."

He wanted to stare at his phone in surprise. That was it? No hesitation? No *sorry, I have other plans*? "You're welcome."

"Chuck's going, too, right?"

"Of course."

"Yay! I can't wait to see y'all. The dream team back in the house!" She laughed.

Michael shook his head, but his heart was lighter than it had been in a while. "It's been too quiet without you around, Pip."

"Ha! I know I'm the loud one, but I'll take that as a compliment."

"You should. It means I've missed you."

"I miss you, too. See you Friday. Gotta go."

Before he could respond in kind, the phone call ended. He slid his cell into his pocket once more and stood there, trying to decipher the emotions he was experiencing.

All of them back in the house again.

"You okay?"

His head shot up, gaze finding Vivian's. "I think so."

Vivian assessed him, her eyes going over his frame. Coming to some sort of a decision, she grabbed a cookie, smoothed frosting all over it, added sprinkles, then offered it to him. "Here. Have a cookie and tell Vivian what's wrong."

Michael was tempted to laugh at her antics, but he was more preoccupied with taking a bite of the sugar cookie. The frosting really did add a nice touch. Once he finished chewing his first bite, he paced around the kitchen.

"It's been almost a full year since we've all been under the same roof. Even though Charles lives nearby, we don't hang out as much as we used to." He frowned. "That's really the main problem. I haven't hung out with any of them as much as I used to. Even when I didn't live in Willow Springs, we got together for our birthdays, just because, whatever." He took another bite.

"Are you sorry you asked them to come?"

"No, but Pippen said something that gave me pause. She thanked me for asking. It made me wonder how much more time I could've had with them if I'd simply asked sooner."

"Hmm..." She leaned her chin on her hand. "Keep talking."

"'Kay. I also wonder why I had to be the one to ask or try at all. Why couldn't they have suggested we get together?" He wanted to throw his hands up in the air, but even he could recognize the dramatics.

"Are you sure they haven't, and you were too oblivious to notice?"

He sighed. Had he been? He racked his memory trying to recall something, *anything*, that would point to that truth, but he couldn't. "No, that's not it. I get that I'm technically head of the family, but I'm not their father. I feel like they should've been willing to reach out or something." He shrugged as frustration gathered.

"I can see your point. I can't imagine the pressure that comes from being the oldest. I am an only child, after all. However, I could imagine looking to an older sibling for guidance if I felt a little lost."

"What about me? What if I feel a little lost?"

Vivian reached out and laid her hand over his. "We all do, Michael. But remember, we have God to be our guide and shine a light when we feel surrounded by darkness."

She squeezed his hand then let go.

And for some reason, he felt the absence more than he'd anticipated.

Chapter Eleven

When Michael said there would be a gingerbread house–making contest at Starts and Stops, Vivian hadn't known what to expect. Her knowledge of that kind of activity was solely gained from watching Hallmark Christmas movies. All she knew was it never looked as easy as it should, and the hero or heroine's gingerbread house was bound to fall apart, depending on which of them needed a dose of humble pie.

But as this *wasn't* a Hallmark movie and there was no hero in sight for her own life story—okay, so she had to ignore the voice that whispered Michael's name as a suggestion—she truly didn't know what to expect. However, Cecelia and Yvonne were going to accompany her. For that, Vivian was thankful. They had been filling Vivian in on their personal lives as they all attempted to get to know one another.

Cecelia was married and had a toddler. Today was her mommy's night out, a weekly escape that she relished, if the repeated giggles and *oh guess what* comments were any indication. Yvonne was a different story, though. Divorced and not looking for a man, she came out of the house to ignore her troubles. When Vivian agreed with her statement on dating, Yvonne's eyes widened in surprise.

"What? What's that look for?" Vivian asked.

"I thought you and Michael were..." Yvonne trailed off as she pointed to where he sat with his brother and sisters.

"Tenant and landlord?" Vivian supplied.

"No," Cecelia and Yvonne said in unison.

"But for real," Yvonne continued. "Y'all aren't dating?"

"No. Like, all-caps no." She cringed. Did that seem a little over-the-top? Was her denial too emphatic?

Cecelia raised an eyebrow while Yvonne tutted.

Vivian blew out a breath. "Nothing can happen."

"Why not?" Cecelia asked quietly.

The words were on the tip of her tongue. It'd be so easy to pull out a sobriety chip and explain why Vivian needed to focus on changing herself from the inside out. How a man would only derail those plans and potentially set her back and have her reaching for a day-one chip all over again. But her relationship with Cecelia and Yvonne was so very valuable—and all too new. How could she risk telling them and receiving their rejection?

"We just can't," she said.

"You don't have to share the reasons," Yvonne said. "But never say never. There's a reason that expression exists."

Vivian glanced over at Michael, watching his head fall back with laughter at whatever his siblings said. She turned back to her own table and picked up another gumdrop to affix to the roof of her gingerbread house. "Maybe so, but he's not for me."

That much had been evident when she'd driven to Jasper for an AA meeting. Her sponsor had found a few locations in the area, encouraging Vivian to join a group.

Jasper had the best times available and was closer than Harrison. Though Harrison did have some online meetings she could attend if necessary.

She'd come a long way, but blowing into the ignition device had reminded her of how much further she had to go. That change didn't happen with a snap of fingers or even instantly after a whispered prayer. God had done wonders for her *and* in her, but Vivian knew she wasn't perfected. If what she'd been reading was true—and obviously the Bible was—then perfection wouldn't happen until she woke in Heaven. Still, she'd do her best to not waylay any steps toward it.

"I'll be praying for whatever hurt you're carrying," Cecelia said. Her lips tilted to the side in sympathy. "I know how hard it is to let things go. People hurt us—"

"Ain't that the truth," Yvonne jumped in.

"And it's not always so easy to forgive," Cecelia continued. "But you have to press forward."

But what if I'm the one who did the hurting? Vivian couldn't ask the question and keep her friends. So she added some sprinkles to the frosting covering the edges of her gingerbread house instead. "Thanks for the encouragement," she murmured. What else could she say? They didn't know the whole truth, and she wasn't willing to lay her secrets before them.

"Of course. It's what friends do." Yvonne smiled. She sat back with a "Ta-da" and spread her hands wide.

"You always make it look so easy," Cecelia groused, staring at the sad state that was her own house. The gingerbread walls were leaning, and the roof barely maintained its position.

"No, I just have the patience to put the pieces together." Yvonne snapped a picture. "This will make a great post on my social media. Even better if I can add a winning ribbon pic."

"They give out ribbons?" Vivian asked.

"Oh, yeah." Yvonne leaned forward. "They have a prize for just about anything. The categories are hilarious. You wait and see."

"I look forward to it," Vivian said.

"Yours looks pretty great for a first timer."

She froze at the deep voice coming from behind her, then twisted in her seat, looking up into his dark eyes. "Michael."

"Hey, Vivian." His gaze drifted behind her. "Cecelia. Yvonne. Nice to see y'all."

"You, too," they chorused.

Vivian begged her cheeks not to betray the heat rising in them. "How's it going with your family?"

"Great. Just thought I'd come over and say hi. Plus, I thought you might want to meet the rest of the crew."

He hitched a finger toward his table. She peeked around his frame to find his family gazing at them with curiosity. "Uh..." She looked at Yvonne and Cecelia who made shooing motions. "Sure."

"Great."

Vivian rose and followed behind Michael, nerves strumming like the beat at a party. What had he told his brother and sisters about her? Surely he'd kept his recounting purely professional, considering they were working on the Christmas Wishes. He couldn't have any other feelings, right?

She stopped, thankful she'd been paying attention to his movements.

"Hey, guys, this is Vivian Dupre. She's the new church secretary I told you about."

Duh. Of course that's how he'd introduce her. She

forced herself not to dwell on the prick of disappointment. Instead, she waved and offered a smile. “Nice to meet y’all.”

“You already know Chuck, but that’s Pippen sitting next to him.”

Vivian nodded at the pretty young woman. She had to be in her early twenties, about a decade younger than herself.

“And sitting across from her is Jordan.”

Jordan grinned, her smile just another striking feature. From the long neck to the pixie haircut, Jordan screamed to be noticed.

“How are you enjoying tonight?” Vivian asked no one in particular.

“It’s our favorite Christmastime activity.” Pippen smiled. Her brown eyes glowed with a mischievous gleam.

“Definitely,” Jordan added with a little sass. “I hear this is your first time ever building a gingerbread house.”

Vivian’s gaze flitted to Michael’s then back to his sister. “It is. It’s been fun.”

“Are you going to the Christmas pageant?”

She’d almost forgotten the church was having a pageant. “I am. Will you still be here?”

Jordan stared at her appraisingly. “Maybe. If I am, I hope we’ll get to know each other better.”

“Well, you know where I live.” Vivian forced a chuckle while mentally berating herself for the awkward conversation. “Um, I better get back to my friends. Have a good evening.”

“You, too, Viv,” Chuck said with a wave.

She turned away and walked back to her seat. Outwardly calm, her mind tried to examine every word that had been exchanged. What did it all mean?

* * *

"Thanks for scaring her away." Michael twisted his lips as he glanced at Jordan.

"I didn't scare her." Jordan threw her hands up in the air.

"Yes, you did," Pippen and Chuck stated.

"See?" Michael popped a piece of fudge in his mouth.

As they had in the past, they'd ordered a bunch of desserts to snack on while building their gingerbread house. In fact, the whole night had seemed reminiscent of old times. They'd laughed, joked and razzed each other over their gingerbread creations.

"Fine," Jordan huffed. "I didn't realize she was so skittish."

"She's not, really," Michael started, trying to think of how to explain Vivian. "I'd say she's more cautious than anything. She waits to see how a person acts before she lets her guard down."

"Is that what she did with you, dear brother?" Jordan asked.

Michael bit back a sigh. "Like I told you earlier, we're just friends." After all, Vivian had said he was in her contact list and let him decorate cookies with her. So what if he kept wondering about being more than friends?

"Do you want there to be something more?" Pippen asked.

"I…" Was she a mind reader? He thought about all his reasons for not wanting a relationship. How much turmoil Alicia had caused and how much better his life was without her. Did that mean saying no to all relationships? Was he better off alone?

"That's a long pause there, Big Mike," Chuck said with a jut of his chin. "You ever think you're protesting too much?"

"I'm not protesting. I'm stating facts. We're friends. We're working together on a church project. That's it."

Chuck turned toward their sisters. "Yet he decorated two Christmas trees with her *and* baked cookies together."

"No, she just let me help decorate the cookies."

Jordan raised her brows while Pippen crossed her arms.

"What? I know those looks mean something."

Pippen laughed. "Of course they do. Just like y'all decking the halls together means something."

"Oh, like we're friends?"

Chuck laughed. "Y'all walked right into that one."

"True," Jordan commented. "But that doesn't mean there's not something more there. Take a chance."

A contemplative look crossed her face. Michael thought of the guy she'd mentioned who had come between her and her roommates. Did Jordan have no regrets?

He rubbed his beard. "Look, I'm not going to take the what-if road. I'm keeping our relationship strictly surface level."

"So you don't have to worry about getting hurt again?" Chuck asked quietly.

Michael wanted to deny it but couldn't. Alicia had done a number on him, and he had no desire to repeat that experience. "Look, coming out of a bad, toxic relationship is draining. Add the fact that Pop died on the heels of that, and I'm just taking it one day at a time. No need to look for something or make hasty judgments."

Like the one where he assumed Vivian Dupre would be another Alicia. But all the time he'd spent with her, the laughter they'd shared over kitchen mishaps, had told him she wasn't even in the same league as Alicia. Vivian Dupre was definitely someone special. Still, Michael didn't want to jump off the diving board and back into the dating pool. He'd rather climb peacefully down the ladder and onto dry ground. Where life was safe and adversity was easy to spot.

Like it was with the Alicia fiasco?

Okay, so he couldn't spot every twist and turn, but at least if he fell, he'd have dry ground catching him. That beat drowning in water any day. And now he was more confused than ever. Did his weird metaphor mean he was ready to date or not?

"For what it's worth," Pippen said, "I like her."

"Me, too," Jordan said. "Even if she did leave a little too fast. Gotta know she has staying power before I give the all clear."

Michael rolled his eyes.

"Vivian's nice, and what she's doing in the community can't be discounted." Chuck took a bite of cheesecake. "She's already made it so the majority of the Christmas Wishes nominees will get their gifts. No one has done that before."

All too true. Michael wasn't sure why his siblings were pushing so hard for him to take another glance at Vivian—especially since he was trying his best to keep her in the friend category. But he could appreciate their care and concern. "I appreciate y'all. Just remember I'm a grown man and know how to take care of myself."

"That's what we all think until life kicks us. We all need a helping hand." Jordan looked away, a frown marring her pretty features.

"You okay, Jay?" Michael murmured.

"Time will tell."

He laid an arm across her shoulders and squeezed. "Talk to me whenever you're ready," he whispered.

"Thanks," she responded just as quietly.

"All right, Willow Springs residents," the Starts and Stops owner's voice rang out.

Ben stood on a footstool, garnering attention from everyone in the restaurant. "It's time to place your creations on the judging table. You'll get a number when you hand in your gingerbread house. Once the judges are done, they'll pick winners for each category. I'll then make the announcement so you can collect your ribbons." He clapped his hands together. "Let's do this in an orderly fashion." He pointed to his left. "This side come on up, one table at a time, and turn in your houses."

While they waited for their turn, Michael gazed at each of his siblings, noting the changes time had wrought since he'd last seen them. He still couldn't believe how easily they'd all come to visit. Or how foolish he felt for not asking them to get together sooner. *Thanks for Vivian's advice, Lord. I might have been too stubborn to make the first move if she hadn't pointed out how simple it could be.*

He turned to Pippen. "How's school going?"

"I'm excited to finish my degree but also don't know what's next." She shrugged as if she didn't have a care in the world.

Michael couldn't tell if she was secretly worried or not stressing until graduation day.

"But you're interning, right?" Chuck asked.

"Yeah, but I'm not sure I really like it. It's a little… boring," she grumbled.

"I think internships are supposed to be boring," Jordan said.

"What about you, Jay?" Chuck asked. "What are you up to? Still working at the bookstore?"

"No. They couldn't afford to keep me."

Michael straightened. Why was he just now hearing this? First guy troubles, now she lost a job? "But you're working now, right?" She'd said work had been busy, hadn't she?

"I've been working at a boutique. They recently opened their doors. Business is booming so far."

Michael wanted to ask a host of questions, but judging from the furrow between Jordan's brows, she had enough on her plate.

"You've always liked fashion," Pippen said.

"Yeah, but it's also not like I thought it would be."

"Nothing ever is," Chuck said.

Three heads swiveled to his, and his eyes widened. "I did *not* mean that like the snark it sounded. I only meant that we all have these grand dreams of how something will be, and when we're in it, it rarely lives up to expectations."

"What has you so down?" Jordan asked.

Chuck shrugged. "Sometimes I think there's more to life but am hard-pressed to figure out exactly what."

"Agreed." Michael offered a fist bump to his brother.

"Our turn," Pippen said, motioning to the judging tables.

They stood and exchanged their gingerbread houses for tickets.

"Think you'll win a category this year?" Jordan asked once they arrived back to their table.

"Nah," Chuck said. "Mine was a mess. Guess I didn't have the brainpower for decorating this year."

"I did, though." Pippen danced in her seat. "I think I should get the most creative." She frowned. "Do they still have that category?"

"Sure hope so," Jordan said.

They chatted quietly until Ben let out a piercing whistle. "All right. Let's take a moment to thank our judges." He gestured toward a group of kids ranging from elementary age to high school.

The restaurant filled with cheers and a round of applause. The kids beamed from the corner they stood in.

"And now, I'll read off the category and the number of the gingerbread house that won. When you hear your number, come up to collect your ribbon."

Michael glanced at his. He'd been awarded number twenty. He glanced at Vivian. *Wonder what she got.* He hoped she won something. Her first contest should be a memorable event.

"The worst gingerbread house goes to number nineteen."

Chuck groaned, then stood with a good-natured grin on his face. Michael laughed and clapped along with the rest of the patrons.

"Guess he was wrong," Pip declared. "He won a category."

When Chuck returned with his ribbon, his eyes looked lighter than they had in a while. Maybe this was just the thing his brother needed to chase away the holiday blues.

Michael laughed once more when Ms. Ann won the house with the most frosting and the sheriff won for most gumdrops. Even Declan Porter, one of the guys always giving guided outdoor tours, won an award—house with the least decorations.

"And last but not least, the best gingerbread house goes to number thirty-five."

Vivian rose, a look of shock on her face.

Michael let out a whistle and clapped.

"A little exuberant for just friends," Jordan mumbled.

"Yeah, yeah." Right now, he could ignore Jordan's ribbing. He was just happy that Vivian would have a good memory to add to her Christmas.

Chapter Twelve

Ugh! The short-term renters across the way had yet to observe quiet hours. The thump of loud music in Vivian's tiny home kept her from hitting a much-needed REM cycle. She rolled over in bed and reached for her cell.

Unlike in a regular home, there was no nightstand to lay her stuff on. Her mattress—though extremely comfortable—rested on the loft floor and not on a box spring. Because of that, she'd purchased wooden containers to add more storage and to rest her electronics on. She tapped on the text icon and found Michael's name. You up?

Unfortunately. I take it you can hear the music too.

Yep.

I'm so sorry. I was hoping they'd quiet down any moment. I'll go talk to them.

Appreciate it. Let me know if I can help.

Not that she really could. She wasn't a cop—*thank You, Lord*—and she didn't have one confrontational bone in her body. But she wanted Michael to know she was here if he needed to talk.

All very friendly.

Thanks. Pray I have the right words to say and that they heed my warning.

Done.

Such an easy prayer to make and one that poured right out of her mouth. There was something so heartwarming in being able to petition God. To know that He would carefully listen and attend to the matters of the heart. That her words mattered to the creator of the universe and no request would be deemed insignificant. Something she hadn't had a lot of growing up.

And right now, Vivian was blessed that Michael let her be part of the prayer team to stand in the gap for him. Someone as young in faith as she was still held a place in the kingdom.

Thank You, Lord.

She rolled onto her back and stared up at the ceiling. Her thoughts turned toward her parents. They still hadn't reached out to her. Vivian was tempted to drive down to Little Rock—if that was allowed under a restricted license—and knock on their door. Or maybe she should keep her distance. Send them a gift with an invitation to come up and visit.

Ugh. She blew out a breath. What was she supposed to do? The thought of respecting their wishes and never speaking to them again chipped off pieces of her heart, leaving holes so that it resembled a colander. How could she mend a relationship when they refused to bridge the gap?

How can I reconcile with my parents, Lord? I've tried

everything I could think of. Please don't say it's not in Your will for our relationship to mend. Please.

Vivian had no idea how she'd handle life without her parents if they stuck to their choice of cutting her out of their lives. Before getting sober, she'd been on the egotistical side. Surely they were merely bluffing, and it was a ploy to get her to pull her act together, she'd thought. Now she desperately hoped for mercy and softness of heart.

She loved them, even if she always felt so very different from them growing up. Her mother and father liked order, while Vivian had bucked against instruction at every turn. Now she saw the need for structure and hated that she'd been so against it. For what reason? Simply to get their attention when she thought they didn't notice her enough? Had she been that vain?

Woop woop.

The sound of a police car had her sitting straight up in bed, heart racing like the moment the steel doors closed against the world for the next six months. She took in a steadying breath, then peeked out the half windows in the loft. Blue strobe lighting streamed from the police car. Vivian's mouth dried as memories of the past filtered through her mind. Was Michael hurt, or had he merely needed police assistance for noise control?

She gulped and reached for her cell with shaky hands. After some deep inhales and exhales, she managed to type out a message. Are you ok? Did something happen?

I'm ok. Talk to you in a minute.

"Thank You, God," she whispered into the still of the night.

She flopped back down onto the bed, heart pounding as her bedroom walls danced with blue beams. All she could think of was the memory of crashing into the cop car. That sinking feeling that she wouldn't be let off with a warning.

Now, in hindsight, Vivian could admit that the punishment had been sorely needed. She would've never gotten sober or found Jesus if it weren't for being sentenced to six months in jail. How odd to be thankful for incarceration, but she was. She just wished she hadn't needed such drastic measures in order to change. That she would have been less stubborn and readily admitted alcohol dependency was the number one problem in her life.

"I won't make the same mistake twice, Lord. I'm sober. I know I can do nothing without You."

She reached for her latest sobriety chip. The number six stood boldly in the center, *months* written in smaller font below. Every time they handed her a new chip, her heart felt lighter and the changes she'd enacted seemed more permanent.

But when would the guilt go away? When could she shake off the shame that reddened her cheeks and broke her heart with mortification? She couldn't even share with Cecelia and Yvonne for fear they'd turn their backs on her and sever all ties like her parents had.

"When will I be good enough, Lord? How many months, *years* will pass before I forget the horrors of that night and the resulting imprisonment?"

A knock pounded on her door, and Vivian jumped. Was it Michael—or worse, the sheriff? She'd been sure to keep her nose clean and steer clear of Sheriff Rawley. She had no desire for anyone in Willow Springs to peek into a past she wanted buried with her old self instead of hanging on like an ankle monitor.

She grabbed a robe to go over her flannel pajamas. Snow was supposed to fall tomorrow, which meant as soon as she opened the door, the cold air would freeze her. It was a good thing her robe was thicker than a luxury hotel's.

After climbing down the ladder, she shuffled over to the front door and opened it.

"Michael…"

"Hey. Is it okay if I come in for a sec?"

"Sure." She stepped back, motioning toward the living space. "Is everything okay? Did they not take your warning under advisement?"

She sat on the other end of the couch, leg jiggling as she waited for his answer. The tinge of blue from the police car's lights had finally left, and only the soft glow of the living room lamp remained. The one she kept on all night to remind herself she was in a tiny home and not a jail cell.

"They turned the music off as soon as I got there."

Of course. Hadn't she noticed the absence of music? She must have been too preoccupied by the lights to realize it. "That's good. Right?" She watched him.

"Yeah—" he rubbed his beard "—but one of the guys started complaining in the background about how they should be allowed to play music as loud as they wanted. Next thing I know, he grabbed his throat and fell over."

"Did he…?" She couldn't bring herself to say it.

"No, he didn't die. Had an allergic reaction, though. Sheriff Rawley has some EMT experience and was closer than the ambulance. He came out and gave the guy a shot from an EpiPen. Rawley ended up getting some information from the other guys before heading to the clinic. Chuck probably got a call to come in and assist the doc." Michael let out a sigh, draping his arms against the back of the couch.

"Does that happen a lot?"

"Yeah. Willow Springs' clinic is pretty small. We're not big enough to have a hospital, but we're close to other towns that do. The clinic rooftop is certified to accept airlifts if someone needs a trauma hospital."

"That's good to know." Not that she planned on needing one.

Michael nodded.

"You look tired." Vivian noted the lines etched into his forehead. She wondered if he had creases surrounding his mouth. The beard hid that information from her.

"I am. I hadn't fallen asleep yet."

"What time is it?" She couldn't remember what her cell had said the last time she'd unlocked it to text him.

He glanced at a wristwatch. "It's two in the morning."

"Oy. You're going to be tired at church tomorrow."

"At least I don't have to worry about a Sunday school teacher calling me out in front of everyone."

She chuckled. "Pastor Randall doesn't seem like the type to draw attention to sleeping congregants." The Sunday school teacher seemed kind.

"He's not. But I used to be so scared of him when I was a kid." Michael laughed. "He seemed larger than life, and Chuck told me he had a direct line to God, which meant punishment could be instantaneous." He shook his head. "Can't believe I fell for that."

Vivian giggled. "Kind of funny. I can see a young kid believing something like that, especially from a brother."

"Yeah, he had me convinced."

She nodded, but her thoughts had taken a turn. Why was Michael here? What was going through his mind?

Suddenly, he sat up, placing his hands on his legs. "Maybe I should go."

"Why did you come?" She winced. "I don't mean that in a bad way. Simply curious."

"No, it's a valid question." He rubbed the back of his neck. "I wanted to vent and found myself on your doorstep. Then when I saw you, I realized maybe you'd fallen asleep once the noise died down. I was going to leave, but you'd already answered."

"Nope. My mind was going a mile a minute, wondering what was going on over there."

"I'm sorry. I promise you we don't have these issues all the time."

"I'm not worried." She wanted to shake him and tell him it was a safe place to relax. Yet somehow that seemed too forward. "I know you run a great place here. I just had too much on my mind."

"What's bothering you?"

"I haven't really said anything, but my parents and I are…" She licked her lips. How could she share the depth of hurt she'd caused without divulging her past? "We're estranged, and I'm really missing them. I think because of the holidays." Or all the unanswered ways she'd tried to communicate.

"Have you reached out to them?"

She nodded. "I have, but nothing. Silence. Silence. Silence." She drew in a breath, hoping her tears would stay away.

"I'm sorry, Vivian."

"I am, too. I don't know what to do anymore." She plucked the edge of her robe.

"Did you think about going to see them?"

"Yes, but I'm not sure that's a good idea. I don't want to risk them closing the door in my face." Or calling the cops. "And I don't know if that's the best move."

"I'm sure you're praying about it."

"I am."

"Then I'll add my prayers to yours. Give it time. He'll answer."

Vivian sniffed, glad her tears hadn't spilled over. "Thanks, Michael."

"Sure. Hey, I just had a thought. After church, let's go to Jimmie's house and gift him his Christmas wish."

"Yes." She'd been praying and thinking about him since she first saw his name on the list. She was so happy they'd bought everything on his list. "Are there any sanitation needs we have to worry about? I know they said his immune system is compromised."

"I'll find out." Michael stood. "Thanks for letting me talk."

"Anytime, friend." She swallowed. That had been an obvious move to keep him under a safe label but seemed totally awkward voiced out loud.

But Michael didn't comment on her odd choice of words. Simply smiled and headed out the door with a wave.

The warm washcloth on his face soothed Michael and helped him wake up. He'd gotten maybe five hours of sleep because he'd spent about a half an hour berating himself for going over to Vivian's house. What had he been thinking, just showing up and expecting her to willingly listen to him?

But she did.

He swallowed. Vivian had simply been kind. He couldn't look for a hidden meaning. Yet listening to her problems with her parents made him realize he needed to reach out to his old boss. Tell him what Alicia had done and resolve that chapter in his life. He'd be kicking himself and drowning in regret if he didn't. That problem would have to wait until tomorrow, though. He didn't want to call his old boss on a personal line or on a Sunday.

"Hurry up in there," Jordan called out, knocking on the door as if Michael hadn't heard her call for the bathroom.

"I'm done, I'm done."

"You decent?"

Michael opened the door with a smirk already on his face for his impatient sister. "I know better than to be indecent with my two sisters around."

"So, you're indecent when we're not around?"

He groaned. "That's not what I meant. I merely meant I'm already dressed."

Jordan stared at his starched button-down shirt. "Looking fancy for church there. Or is it a particular lady you're hoping to attract?"

"Jay, we're going to present a gift after church. I thought I'd go to the extra effort for the people I'll be seeing later."

"Sure, brother, sure." She pushed him out of the bathroom and closed the door. "You like her!"

Michael shook his head and started toward the kitchen. He needed another cup of coffee before they left for church. When he got close to the kitchen, he saw Pippen drinking from a mug. *His* mug.

"Morning, Pip."

She grinned. "Hey, Michael. Thanks for making a cup of coffee."

He nodded, but his face must have given away his thoughts, because Pippen's expression fell.

"This was your cup, wasn't it?"

"It was—" he swallowed "—but I already had one. You're fine, Pip."

"Really?"

The uncertainty in her voice undid him. He walked up to her and gave her a hug. "What's going on with you? You seem down."

"No, no. I'm fine." She stepped back and showed him a bright smile. "I am."

No one in the Wood family seemed fine. "You know you can talk to me, right?"

"Yeah," she responded softly. "*If* I ever did have a problem, I'd try and solve it myself, though."

"Sometimes we need help." Wasn't that what they'd been telling him? Wasn't that what he wanted for himself? Help.

"Yes, but sometimes you want to know you can stand on your own two feet."

Michael held back a groan. As much as he hated the thought of Pip struggling with something, he understood the sentiment all too well. "Okay, but you know where help is if you ever need it."

"I do know that." She squeezed his arm. "Want me to make you a cup?"

"Nah. We gotta get to church."

Jordan walked up to them. "Then I'm ready just in time."

It was weird walking into the Springs Bible Church with his two sisters. Michael almost expected his parents to be whispering over his shoulder, keeping a supervising eye on them. Some days their absence stung, and other days it packed a wallop like a horse's kick. Walking into church to the pew Chuck had saved for them made the moment feel bittersweet. They would continue on the legacy their parents had left them. Coming together for the weekend had done wonders for Michael's spirit, and by the time they stood and walked out at the end of service, he was ready to spread the blessings.

"Are y'all leaving right now?" he asked Jordan and Pippen.

"No. Chuck is taking us to lunch, then we'll head back home to pack. You think you'll be back in time to see us off?" Pippen asked.

"Definitely. Vivian and I are just going to drop some gifts off and come back to Simplicity afterward."

"Maybe we should have lunch at home, then." Jordan suggested. "Wait for you and Vivian?"

He hesitated. The urge to say *yes* came swiftly, but were his sisters trying to push him and Vivian together? "I'll ask her if she's up to it."

"Up to what?" Vivian asked as she walked over to them. "Sorry. I heard Jordan say something about waiting for us?"

"For lunch," Chuck volunteered. "Jordan and Pippen offered to cook." He threw a smirk their way. "And we thought y'all would be finished with Christmas Wishes by the time they're finished."

"Lunch sounds good. If you don't mind," Vivian said.

"We really don't." Pippen eyed Michael. "Do you, big brother?"

"Of course not." He wanted to rub the heat climbing his neck. Good thing his brown skin hid telltale hints.

"Great. See y'all in a bit," Jordan said.

The three left him alone with Vivian. "You ready?"

"I am. You?"

"Sure. My truck is loaded with the gifts, and I have hand sanitizer. His dad will give us masks once we're there."

"Great."

They didn't talk much as they walked to the parking

lot. Vivian waved to a couple of people who called out a goodbye greeting. Finally, they were in the truck and headed to Jimmie's house. Michael really hoped that the kid loved the home office setup they'd been able to put together. Someone had donated a desk, another person had donated a desktop computer and the last person donated a gaming chair. All they'd had to buy with Christmas Wishes funds were a noise-canceling headset and supplies including a school planner and pencils.

Michael parked in the driveway and turned to Vivian. "How should we do this? Unload everything first or knock first?"

She laughed. "Probably knock first."

"Good idea." He grinned as she continued to chuckle softly as she got out of the truck.

They strolled up the walkway, then Vivian knocked. "I hope they're home. I so want this to be a good surprise."

"It will be." He prayed.

The door opened, and a woman looked at them expectantly. All of a sudden, Michael knew who she was. They'd gone to high school together. "Hey, CJ. This is Vivian. She's been helping me with the Christmas Wishes project."

"Nice to meet you. And to see you again, Michael."

"Likewise." He swallowed. Why did this feel so awkward?

"Um, how can I help y'all?"

Michael forgot the dad was keeping it a surprise for the son and his wife.

"Jimmie was nominated for the Christmas Wishes program," Vivian started, "so we were wondering how we should deliver his gift."

CJ gasped. "Are you serious?" She tucked a strand of curly hair behind her ear, but it sprang right up.

"Yes, ma'am. It's in the truck."

"I'll get Craig to help you unload it. If you need the help, that is."

"I sure do." Michael said.

He and Craig unloaded everything into the living room while CJ called for her son. Jimmie froze when he spotted Michael and Vivian, wearing their masks.

"Hey, Jimmie, this is Mr. Wood and Ms. Dupre. They're running Christmas Wishes this year," CJ said.

Jimmie's eyes roamed over Michael and Vivian, then the boxes in the middle of living room. His eyes grew wide. "Someone nominated me?" he whisper-shouted.

"They did, son," Craig said. "Go ahead. Go on and open it."

Jimmie tore into the wrapping paper, shredding it off the sides and shouting when he saw the picture of the computer. "I got a computer! How cool."

Craig turned to Michael. "I thought it'd be a desk or something."

"Just wait," Michael murmured.

Craig and CJ watched as their son unveiled the desk and all the other trappings they'd received for him.

"This is too much," CJ mumbled, tears tracking down her face. "Surely others needed to be gifted more than us."

"Please don't worry," Vivian stated. "I assure you, no one will be overlooked."

CJ wrapped Vivian in a hug, then turned to hug Michael next. "Thank y'all so much. So, so much."

"It's our pleasure." Vivian glanced up at Michael and gave a thumbs up.

Michael couldn't help but smile behind his mask. Watching Jimmie's and his parents' reactions was the best way Michael had ever ended a church morning. The. Best.

Chapter Thirteen

The Wood siblings were an interesting mix. They told inside jokes and had a camaraderie that obviously came with growing up together and being related. Still, an underlying tension and strain ran through the room, without any acknowledgment from them. At least, not in Vivian's presence. So she kept mum as well.

The other odd thing—she had the distinct impression they were assessing her. Like they wanted to know if she was good enough. But for what? Surely not for Michael's sake. Wouldn't he have already informed them they were merely friends? Coworkers on a bad day?

She took a bite of the biscuit Jordan had made. The lunch was more of a brunch, with several delicious dishes to choose from. Chuck had made sausage gravy to accompany the biscuits, while Pippen had made a shrimp salad and mac and cheese. Vivian couldn't pass up the biscuits—bread was life, after all—so she opted to have some of everything. Today was not the day to eat a light meal.

Her taste buds were delighted. "This is all so good," Vivian said.

"Agreed." Michael gestured to his plate. "Sorry I didn't help."

"Don't be." Pippen tucked her long black hair behind her ear. "You let us stay the weekend and upend your peaceful existence."

Chuck snorted.

"Well, you didn't invite us over, Charles." Jordan stared at him as if daring him to disagree.

"Next time." He shrugged.

"Maybe it's time you settle down so you won't want for company." Michael smirked before taking a sip of his coffee.

Vivian felt like she was missing another joke.

"After you settle down, brother."

"'Nough of that." Jordan waved a hand in the air. "Y'all gotta tell me what you've been up to before Pip and I hit the road."

"Just working at the clinic," Chuck said. "Work, eat, sleep, repeat."

Michael laughed. "Same for me. Though sometimes I forget a meal here or there."

"For shame," Vivian chimed in. "I never miss a meal."

"You're also within walking distance of the general store and can pack a lunch," Chuck said.

"True. But someone is always bringing in food to church, so we usually have that." It was awesome to see the kindness of the community in action on a daily basis. "Though sometimes I have a salad on standby."

"What about y'all two?" Chuck asked. "How's life in Fayetteville?"

The ladies exchanged a glance, some unspoken conversation going on between them. Jordan set her fork down and answered first. "I'm not happy. My roommate situation is rotting fast. But since I have a job that pays my bills, I guess I have no room for complaints."

"The guy thing?" Michael asked.

Vivian held her breath. Jordan was having men trouble? She prayed it wasn't a volatile situation.

Jordan shrugged a shoulder. "It's not just that. I've been wanting a change anyway. Only switching jobs didn't seem to help any." She looked down at her plate as if lost in thought.

Vivian's heart went out to Jordan. She was obviously going through difficult times right now. She said a quick prayer and made note to say a longer one when she was alone.

"The offer to come back home stands," Michael stated.

"We'll see." Her lips flattened as the mood in the room turned downward.

"What about you, Pip? How's everything?" Michael asked.

"I'm worried about life after college. I feel like academia keeps you in a bubble from the real world."

"Any boyfriends we should know about?" Chuck asked, pointing a finger between Pip and Jordan.

"No," Jordan responded swiftly.

"Same," Pip said.

All the Wood siblings were single? Something told Vivian there was more there than anyone was saying.

"Where are you from, Vivian?" Jordan asked.

Good thing she'd already finished chewing her food or Vivian might have choked on that piece. "Little Rock."

"Nice. So still an Arkansas girl. I couldn't tell, because your accent is subtle."

Vivian grinned. "My mom's doing. She taught me to be a genteel Southern woman."

"But were you?" Pippen asked.

"I am now." Her lips quirked in a grin as she remembered some of her antics. Climbing trees was a no-no according to her mom but had been relaxing for Viv.

"Very vague, but we can read between the lines, Viv." Chuck's lips twitched with barely contained amusement.

"I've changed, but I was very much a stereotypical daughter growing up. Butting heads with my mom, trying to go to parties as a teen." She sighed. "I wanted her attention but went about it the wrong way."

"Sometimes life lessons are hard to learn." Michael nudged her softly with his elbow. "Thankfully, we can all claim a little foolishness in our youth."

"What did you do that was ever so foolish?" Pip asked, a look of incredulity on her face.

She kind of looked like a ventriloquist puppet at the moment, Vivian thought.

"He stole Pop's truck one year," Chuck answered.

Vivian gaped. "Really?"

Michael rubbed the back of his neck. "That was very reckless. And I wouldn't exactly use the word *stole*."

"Joyrides are still stolen vehicles when your folks don't give you permission," Chuck said.

"Yes, but Pop didn't report it as a crime. Just told the police to find me safely." Michael turned to Vivian. "I thought because he let me ride it around our land that it would be okay to drive to a girl's house. It wasn't."

All the women laughed.

"Why don't I remember this?" Jordan asked.

"That was the year you were mooning over Ty," Chuck said.

Jordan covered her face, groaning with embarrassment.

Vivian laughed at their antics. "Y'all have a great family." It's what she'd wanted growing up. People who knew you, cared about you and still joked around.

They nodded.

"We really do," Michael said.

After Vivian finished her food, she offered to do the dishes.

"No way," Pippen said. "You're our guest."

"Are you sure? I'd like to clean up anyway." Do something to reciprocate the kindness they'd shown her since they first met.

"No. Go home and rest or whatever it is you do on a Sunday afternoon."

Sit outside and enjoy my freedom. Vivian swallowed. "If you're sure."

"I am. Michael," Pippen yelled.

"Hmm?" He walked toward the kitchen counter.

"Walk Vivian home."

"You don't have to." She hated that her cheeks always flushed around him. "You know I won't get lost."

He laughed. "You won't, but I don't mind escorting you. I can check on the guys from last night."

"Oh, yeah. Definitely do that." Of course he had a legit reason to walk over to the tiny homes.

As they headed downstairs and out through the general store, Vivian looked at Michael, admiring the steady strength he always seemed to exude, the kindness he showed other people. When they first met, she'd thought him brusque and a little standoffish. Now she wondered how much of that could be chalked up to an awkwardness between strangers or even a defense mechanism to keep people at arm's length. She could understand both.

"Thanks for today. It was great to see Jimmie's face, and the meal will have me taking a nap in a few minutes," Vivian said.

"I think we all wish for a Sunday nap."

"Do you ever take a rest?" Vivian stared up at him, glad the sun wasn't blocking her view.

Michael sighed. "Not really. I'm just glad the general store is open only a few hours on Sunday. Most folks understand, because they're at church as well." He glanced at his watch. "And it's almost time to open up shop."

"Take it easy when you can." Vivian slid her hands into her pockets, waffling on the idea that sprang to mind. "Um, if you ever need an extra hand on the weekends, I could help."

His eyes lit up. "Really? I can pay you."

"No." She shook her head, heart pounding at the implications. "Just to help out. I don't need to be paid." She stepped backward. A foot closer to safety. "Talk to you later."

She swung around and unlocked the door of her tiny home, closing it swiftly behind her. If Michael tried to pay her, wouldn't he find out about her criminal record? She squeezed her eyes shut. *Stupid move, Viv. Stupid move.*

What just happened?

The urge to scratch his head and knock on Vivian's door had Michael stepping forward. But knowing it was almost time to open the general store and needing to check on his short-term renters kept him from doing so. He'd have to ponder her odd reaction to payment later.

He walked across the lawn to the guys who'd made such a ruckus yesterday. He hoped their friend was well. According to their online reservation, they'd be here another week before heading home. Hopefully they wouldn't blast music anymore. The homes were too close together for such noise.

Michael knocked on the door and waited for any sound of movement or life in the house. He knocked again. Maybe they hadn't returned from the hospital? He huffed and walked away. He needed to open the store, say goodbye to Jordan and Pippen, and think about how wonderful lunch had been with all of them. *Including Vivian.*

He didn't want to admit it, but he was beginning to wish he hadn't put himself in the friend zone. Vivian made him believe in second chances and that a relationship with another person could be genuine. The stuff she'd shared with him, the vulnerability in letting him know of the estranged relationship between her and her parents, had tugged something loose in him. He wanted to comfort her and be there for her. To let her know she wasn't alone and he cared about what she was going through.

But then that meant *he* would have to be vulnerable. Was he ready for that? He still had the whole mess with Alicia to clear up before he could move on—break free from the invisible chains tethering him to her. Once he did that, maybe then he could sit Vivian down and see what she thought about going on a date, seeing where they could go.

And perhaps he should say a few thousand prayers that the feelings weren't one-sided and ask if God even wanted him to be with Vivian. Something he hadn't done with Alicia and regretted. *So, what's stopping you now?* Good point. Guess his prayer muscles were a little rusty. He'd been trying to pray daily since Vivian first brought up his lack of seeking God first—*after* he got over the stubbornness of admitting she was right.

Lord, uh, I'd like to go out with Vivian. I feel like she's completely different from Alicia and wouldn't bring me down but lift me up. I love how she loves You and feels like You always listen. I love that she's an encourager and kind to everyone she meets. But what I don't know is how You feel about the two of us together, as more than friends. He swallowed. Why did this have to feel so awkward?

He stopped by the side of his house and bowed his head.

Please give me wisdom on how to move forward—whether that's as friends or with hopes we can be more if she's willing to take a chance on me. Thanks for listening. Amen.

He rounded the store in time to see Chuck exit the front doors. "Leaving?"

Chuck turned and nodded. "Going to relax before the workweek starts."

Michael gave his brother a clap on the back. "Understand. It was great hanging out with you this weekend."

"Mean that?" Chuck asked quietly.

"Honest."

Chuck nodded once more, sliding his hands in his jacket pocket. "I enjoyed myself, too, Big Mike."

"Don't be a stranger."

Chuck smirked. "Likewise."

With a wave, Michael strolled into the store and flipped the Closed sign to open. He paused at the sound of footsteps and looked over his shoulder to see Pippen and Jordan carrying luggage.

"Vivian get home okay?" Pip asked.

Michael nodded, rolling his eyes for good measure.

"Guess it's our turn now," Jordan said.

Michael hugged Jordan, then Pippen. "I'm so glad y'all came. Will you be back for Christmas?"

"Definitely," Pippen said. "All I'm doing is working

right now. I already requested Christmas Eve and Christmas Day off."

"Same," Jordan said.

Relief flooded through him. There would be another family get-together. "Great. Then I'll see y'all for Christmas."

"Be sure to invite Vivian." Jordan winked.

"'Bye, ladies."

They laughed all the way out the general store door. Michael sighed. He didn't know what was going on with those two, but he sincerely hoped Jordan moved back. He'd need to call her when no one else was around to listen in on the conversation. Maybe even call Pip, too, if she didn't want to stay in the city. He'd never turn them away. If they didn't want to live with him upstairs, they could always stay in one of the tiny homes.

Regardless, he was glad they knew they always had a home here. Something about this weekend had been healing. There was still some strain between all of them, but Michael now had hope it would fade away with time and togetherness.

The door chimed, and Michael set out to work. He didn't yet have a plan for decreasing his workload, but maybe he'd take Vivian up on her offer if she truly meant it. Though he couldn't in good conscience let her work for free.

But how much can you afford?

He wasn't sure, but that was something he needed to figure out before he turned to her for help. Until then, he'd ask for God's provision and continue plodding through.

Chapter Fourteen

The wind nipped through Vivian's hair as she hurried up the church steps and into the atrium. Heat greeted her with a whoosh as the doors closed behind her. She scanned the vestibule, searching for any familiar faces. Of course, since this was Willow Springs, that meant she saw a lot of people she'd become acquainted with. What she wanted to spy was a friendly face in the sea of people here for the pageant.

Her cheeks heated at the sight of Michael. When had that become a habit? She'd been so firm on sticking to the one-year relationship-free commitment that she'd been able to ignore Michael's good looks upon first meeting. But the longer she knew him, the more she learned about him and the more she saw his kindness in action, the harder it was to ignore the feelings cropping up in her heart. She swallowed as someone shifted and Sheriff Rawley became visible.

As much as she wanted to say hi to Michael, she didn't want to get into such close range of Willow Springs' sheriff. What if he asked about her past? Would he sense she didn't divulge the whole picture?

Just as she was about to change direction, Michael

locked eyes with her then waved her over. She gulped as she put one foot in front of the other while practically begging God to make the sheriff find someone else to talk to. Alas, he grinned and nodded at Vivian as if they were good friends.

The contents of her stomach soured, and she squeaked out a greeting.

Michael's brow raised. "Everything okay?"

Vivian cleared her throat. "Yep. Yes." She forced a smile. "Hi, Sheriff."

"Ms. Dupre. Nice to officially meet."

Her palms grew clammy at his word choice. *Officially* officially or *unofficially* officially? She blinked. "You, too." That was polite, right?

"How are you enjoying our humble town?"

"I love Willow Springs." That she could answer instantly and without reserve. The people here were so welcoming, and the pace of life was just what she needed. She said as much.

"Couldn't agree with you more. I tried moving away and enjoying a faster way of life." He shrugged. "Guess this place will always have my heart."

"Mine, too," Michael added. "It's easier to breathe out here."

"Might be the fresh air," she quipped.

The men chuckled, and she slowly let out a breath. So far so good. Still, her deodorant's powers were being tested and her fight-or-flight system was primed for flight. If he so much as said boo, she'd probably jump straight up like a cartoon cat clinging to the roof.

Piano music filtered into the foyer, and Vivian tilted her head to decipher the melody. "What's that song?"

"Ah, that would be the get-your-rear-in-gear instrumental Mrs. Phillips likes to play to get people's attention," Michael said with a smile.

"I'm going to go find a seat." Sheriff Rawley shook Michael's hand and tipped his imaginary hat to Viv.

She had to admit, she breathed easier the moment he stepped away from her.

"Want to sit with me?" Michael asked.

"Yes. That sounds like fun." And she would ignore the blush trying to show. This wasn't a date, merely two friends who were attending a small-town Christmas pageant...with the rest of the townsfolk. Besides, she couldn't let him sit alone since none of his siblings could make the show.

Michael ushered them down the aisle, gesturing toward a couple of empty seats in the process. They took their places, and he immediately reached for his phone, opening a Bible app. Vivian leaned close. "Is there something I should know?" she whispered.

"Oh, I like to follow along in Luke, just to orient myself with what plays out on stage."

Vivian opened her print Bible to the chapter Michael pointed out. Soon, however, the production started, and her attention became riveted to the stage. Never before had Vivian seen something so adorable as the young children dressed up on the church stage. There were lambs, wise men, Mary and Joseph, and a cute baby whose nap had been timed perfectly as he lay in a makeshift manger.

A set of two-dimensional animals in a barn had been constructed and laid out where the worship team's instruments usually sat. Lines were forgotten—to the audience's amusement—and some kids burst into tears, setting off a chain reaction.

Yet the reason why they celebrated Christmas was

clear to all. The love of a God Who would send down His only child for atonement of sin. Vivian teared up as the wise men laid their gifts at the baby's feet. She was very aware that it was a church congregant's child and not the actual baby Jesus, but her emotions and heart were caught up in the imagery.

A tissue came into her view, and she blindly reached for the material to mop at her face. It was a good thing she was no longer heavy-handed with makeup. That, and her waterproof mascara actually proved to be effective.

Michael curled an arm around her shoulders, gave a quick squeeze, then settled his hand back on his thigh. Vivian froze, blinking rapidly now from shock and not from trying to stem the flow of tears. Had that just happened? Had he really offered her a hug? And why was she so shocked by the comfort? Michael was a gentle, sweet man. Of course he would try and keep her from blubbering like the kid dressed as a lamb.

She drew in a deep breath and blew it out. As much as she wanted to keep her feelings under lock and key, she couldn't deny how Michael's personality had hooked her heart like a fish to bait.

What am I going to do, Lord? Because if she really wanted to have a chance with Michael, she needed to come clean about her past and see if he would ever be able to overlook it. Yet the thought had her stomach heaving to and fro like a duck in a hurricane. Could she really be vulnerable, reveal all her past mistakes and pray that somehow Michael would understand without casting judgment?

She stared at the scene on the stage and let out a breath. No, she didn't know how she would bring herself to be honest, but she'd have to try sooner rather than later.

* * *

Michael smiled as the children all stood and bowed to the applause. He rose with the rest of the audience, clapping for the production. This was one of his favorite things to watch in the Christmas season. He wasn't a big movie watcher—frankly, he didn't have much time to sit for a couple of hours. But he always came to the pageant to cheer on the town's children and remember why he believed. Because the savior of the world was someone you willingly focused on. Pausing his everyday duties and taking the moment to refocus his mind on why he believed in God was so very needed.

Especially since he'd been praying faithfully on what to say to Vivian. He felt cautious when it came to opening up and asking her on a date. Whether that caution stemmed from past wounds with Alicia or a yellow light from the Lord, he couldn't tell. He continued to pray for clarity and wisdom, and so far, he'd had multiple opportunities to get to know Vivian better in a nondate setting. But did that mean he had the green light to be intentional and ask her out?

Yeah, sometimes his own thoughts exhausted him.

Michael stepped into the aisle and motioned for Vivian to proceed him. Slowly they shuffled out of the sanctuary with the rest of the people. He slid his hands into his jacket pockets, mind racing. Should he ask her out? Casually suggest a bite to eat?

They didn't have any Christmas Wishes gifts planned until tomorrow evening. So there went that excuse. And he was very much aware he was reaching for excuses to keep her in his company. His face heated. He never felt this way over a woman—as if he had to give her his best, not for egotistical reasons, but because she deserved it.

As they entered the outer room, Michael looked down at Vivian. "You going home?"

"I don't know. I thought about walking to the Sassy Spoon for some dessert. Someone said Ma Spooner makes a delicious bread pudding."

"Oh, she does." His mouth watered in anticipation. "That sounds like a great idea. Want some company?"

"Sure." She smiled.

He let out a sigh of gratitude. Maybe tonight he could figure out the words that matched his thoughts and emotions. See what she was thinking on the more-than-friends factor. Of course, he needed to brace himself in case it was all one-sided. That would definitely be mortifying to discover. *Lord, please go before me and pave the way if this is Your will.*

He cleared his throat. "Up for a walk or do you want to drive?"

"A walk sounds nice."

He motioned toward her head. "How come you never wear a beanie? Doesn't your head get cold?" He didn't consider himself a wimp, but when that wind whipped through, a beanie kept the rest of him from shivering.

"It's my arms that always get chilled. It was one reason I bought this jacket in your store. I don't mind if the rest of me gets a little chill as long as my arms are good."

"Funny how we differ."

She peered up at him. "That's a good thing, though, right?"

"I think so." He swallowed, heart thumping. "Do you always have a lot in common with your…friends?" Not the word he wanted to use, but maybe he needed to warm up to the real deal.

Vivian shrugged. "I'm not sure I ever gave it much thought. I just enjoy being around others, especially those within the church community. I find most of them bolster my spirits more than people from my past."

"You don't talk about your past much. Why is that?"

Silence fell between them, but Michael waited patiently as they strolled toward the Sassy Spoon. He wanted Vivian to trust him with whatever she needed his trust for.

"It's a very difficult situation. One I haven't fully worked through."

"If you ever want to talk, I hope you know I would listen."

Vivian stared up at him, biting her lip. Then she spoke softly in the night. "Would you?"

Chills ran up his arms. Was she still unsure of him? As a friend…or more? "I would."

"I'll keep that in mind, then."

They walked inside the restaurant, and Michael guided them to the booth where he always sat. He didn't need to peek at the menu, since bread pudding had already been decided. As soon as a server stepped in front of their table, he placed his order and asked for a hot chocolate as well.

"That sounds great. Same for me," Vivian said.

"We're ordering the same foods? That makes us best friends, right?" He winked at her.

She ducked her head—he hoped it was to hide a blush and not because she was irritated.

"You might be the best friend I have in Willow Springs." She met his gaze. "Though Ms. Ann might disagree."

He laughed. "She's everyone's friend. She collects us all like strays."

"I believe it." Vivian gave an answering grin. "I definitely felt like a stray moving up here."

"I'm glad you did—move here, I mean. It's been great getting to know you." He paused. This was it. He should just go out and say it. Ask her on a true date.

"Here y'all go. Two bread puddings and two hot chocolates." Their server placed the dishes before them. "Y'all need anything else?"

A defibrillator? Because she'd come out of nowhere and drained him of the courage he'd ramped up. "I'm good. Thanks."

"Me, too," Vivian said. "Shall I say grace?" Her eyes held a vulnerability.

"Of course. I'd love that."

"Heavenly Father, thank You for delicious dessert and friends to share it with. Amen."

"Amen," he whispered.

Because after that soft proclamation of him being a friend, could he really tip the scales and ask her out? Maybe they just needed more time to adjust to one another. Maybe his thoughts were going too fast, too soon.

So he took a big bite of the bread pudding and focused on keeping the conversation light and friendly. If they were meant to be, he'd just have to pray their time would come and those green lights would be obvious.

Chapter Fifteen

Last night Vivian had slept the whole night through. No loud music, no jumping at the slightest sound. She'd finally adjusted to life in Willow Springs and had awakened feeling refreshed and ready to start another week as the Springs' secretary. This would be Ms. Ann's last week working, and Vivian would miss her. At the same time, she was so happy the older woman would be surrounded by family. Ms. Ann's movers should have come over the weekend to load everything up and take it to their new place near their first grandchild.

Vivian locked up the house and slid her purse over her shoulder as she walked toward the parking lot. The snowstorm the forecaster had called for over the weekend had bypassed them and headed for Missouri instead. Vivian wasn't upset, but she wished the temperature had risen a bit if there wasn't going to be any white precipitation falling from the sky.

She unlocked her car door and slid her purse onto the passenger seat, then sat and buckled up. Her stomach tensed as she stared at the device that would grant her permission to start her car. With dread, she put her mouth around the tube and blew just as a shadow moved over her. The device lit green, and she straightened to peer out the driver side window.

Her jaw dropped in shock as Michael stared at her with horror in his eyes. She wrestled with her seat belt, frantically reaching for the door handle, but he'd already started walking away. She pushed the door open.

"Michael, wait. I can explain."

He froze, his body tense.

Lord, I have no idea how to explain. "Michael?" She stopped behind him, hand poised to lay a palm on his back. She changed her mind as he turned to face her. The look of anguish in his eyes had her stepping back. "Michael…" she whispered.

"Tell me that wasn't a sobriety device you were just breathing into." His words were terse, each spoken with a clipped ending.

She gulped. "I can't."

His eyes squeezed shut while hers welled with tears.

"I'm so very sorry. I should have said something sooner."

"You think?"

"I was afraid to lose your friendship." She licked her lips as she fought for the words. "Especially after finding out how your dad died."

Grief stole across his features so quick and fierce that she bit back a gasp. The pain in her chest felt like her heart was splitting in two, and it was all she could do not to fall at his feet and beg forgiveness. Not that she had anything to do with his father dying, but she felt guilty just the same.

"Please, Michael. I'm sorry. I didn't know how to share this part of my past."

"What do you mean, your past? I just saw you blow into that tube!" He flung an arm toward her car, indignation carving his features into granite.

"I promise you, it's my past. I was just so ashamed to talk about it. But I've changed so much since they ordered that on my car. That's not who I am anymore."

He held up a hand. "I don't want to hear it."

"But if you'd let me explain—"

"No, thanks." Bitterness tinged every word. "Come the new year, you need to find a new place to live."

"Michael." She gaped. "I..."

"Leave. Go to work and continue pretending to be some paragon of virtue where the good Lord fixes everything and you can bless people's heart to death."

He's just hurting—he doesn't mean it. But the expression on his face and the way he walked away without a backward glance told Vivian otherwise. Tears streamed down her face and her breath came in spurts as she walked back to her car. Enduring the humiliation of blowing into the device all over again as she pictured the look on Michael's face added to the pain, and she sobbed her way to work. By the time she put the car in Park in front of the church, her makeup had made a horrifying watercolor palette on her face. She dug around in her glove box for tissues. She didn't want to have to explain why she was crying. Not when her heart felt so raw and one kind word away from bursting again.

Vivian walked into the foyer and headed for the offices. As soon as she entered the secretary's office, the smile on Ms. Ann's face fell and she came to an abrupt stand.

"What happened, sugar?"

Vivian bit her lip to keep the tears from coming. "I'm okay," she croaked.

"Oh, sweet girl, you most certainly are not." Ms. Ann wrapped an arm around her shoulders and guided her to the couch in the office. "Tell me what happened."

She drew in a breath, trying to find the strength to just

tell the truth. "Michael discovered something about my past. Something I've been hiding." She looked down at her hands. "I'm a recovering alcoholic."

"How did he find that out?"

Vivian stared at Ms. Ann. That's it? That's all she wanted to know?

"Vivian?"

"Uh, he saw me breathing into the interlock device on my car."

"I see. Did you try and explain why you hadn't shared that part of your past with him?"

She nodded. "He didn't want to hear it. Told me to find some other place to live by New Year's."

Ms. Ann drew back. "He can't do that unless your lease ends then."

"It doesn't. I signed for six months." But did that really matter?

"Then he definitively can't kick you out without good cause or he breaks the lease." Ms. Ann's lips pursed and lines framed her face, increasing the visual irritation.

"Honestly, where I live isn't my biggest concern. I've been so worried about how people would react if they found out I've been holding on to this secret that it's determined how I go about my days. Where I park or what I say to help maintain the secrecy. All of it turned me into a jumble of knots."

Ms. Ann tutted. "That's the problem with trying to shut up those skeletons. That kind of stress will turn you inside out. What I don't understand is why you felt the need to go to such lengths. Aren't you sober?"

"Yes, ma'am. Have been for almost seven months." Vivian straightened. That was something no one could take away. Her commitment to a new life was evident in the chips she collected.

"Congratulations, dear."

Warmth filled Vivian at Ms. Ann's kindness. Not to mention that the woman hadn't batted an eye at her admission. "Thanks, Ms. Ann."

"Don't thank me. I suspect hard work on your part and the good Lord's grace are the ones responsible for your success."

She nodded. "Definitely God's grace." She'd be nothing without His work in changing her.

"Don't discount your desire to change for the better, either."

"I don't. But how do I know everyone will see it that way?"

"Vivian Dupre, where do you think you are?"

She eyed the room. "The Springs Bible Church."

"At *church*." Ms. Ann nodded. "That's right. And who goes to church?"

"Believers."

"Sinners in need of grace, child. The problem with our eyes is we think the cute dresses and nice shirts mean the person underneath is as clean as their laundered clothing." She tsked. "Instead, we should walk in here with the spiritual knowledge that we have *all* fallen short and every one of us needs God's grace and forgiveness."

"Really?" Vivian sniffed. "I mean, I know that mentally, I suppose. But really?"

Ms. Ann sat back, resting her hands on her stomach. "Ever hear the Bible proverb about the brawling wife? I think that's how the King James version puts it."

"The one about being on the housetop or something like that?"

"Exactly. That was me in the early days of my marriage. I drove my husband up a wall at every turn."

Vivian's mouth dropped. "But you're one of the sweetest women I know."

"*Now* I am, because God transformed my heart. Plus I was willing to do the work to adjust my bad behavior and attitude. But *sweet* surely wasn't a word anyone would use to describe me in my twenties." A reminiscent look clouded Ms. Ann's gaze. "It's due to nothing but God's grace that I'm still married, and my husband chose to forgive me. You take the time to join a Bible study or make friends in this town and you'll see we all have our own pasts. Nobody's trying to throw stones, and if they are, it's their heart that needs working on, not yours."

"You really believe that?" Vivian desperately wanted to, but fear gripped her.

"I know so, Vivian. You hold that chin up and exhibit the fruits of a repentant spirit. And know that you're not the only one who has a past they aren't proud of. But because of Jesus's work on the cross, you no longer have to be ashamed of it."

Vivian threw her arms around Ms. Ann. "Thank you so much."

"Anytime, sweet girl. Anytime."

An alcoholic?

No matter how many times Michael repeated the information in his head, his brain couldn't make sense of it. How hadn't he seen the signs? Better yet, how had he never seen Vivian blow into that device before? All the times he'd offered to drive, had she accepted in order to prevent the scrutiny of her condition? Was this the *real* reason her parents wanted nothing to do with her?

He'd been duped again. Fooled by another woman who wanted to hide a secret agenda—or, in Vivian's case, a shameful past. He rubbed the back of his neck as he continued pacing back and forth in the general store.

He couldn't help but think this was why he kept feeling caution around her. He'd feel like a bigger fool if he'd gone through the plan of asking her out last night. But instead of feeling like he'd dodged a bullet, his heart felt the gaping wound of the shot.

Before he could form another thought, his cell rang. He groaned at the caller ID. He'd called his former boss this morning but been informed by the secretary that Grady had been in a meeting. Letting his mind circle around the business of Vivian's betrayal would have to wait until he dealt with this call.

"Michael Wood, I heard you were the first phone call of my day."

"Hey, Grady. How've you been?"

"Fine and dandy. Yourself? Enjoying small-town life?" Grady always did have a good-natured humor.

"Sure am." Up until Vivian's betrayal.

"Bummer. I thought you were calling because you want your old job back. Which I'd happily give you—just say the word."

"Are you serious?" Michael straightened. After the way he'd left?

"Sure am. Alicia…" The man blew out a breath. "Why didn't you tell me what she did?"

"How did you find out?"

"Well, no thanks to you, it took us a little longer to discover the depth of her deceit."

Michael ran a hand down his face, but it didn't erase the wince. "I'm sorry. I was so shocked by the whole bait and switch. I didn't know what to do, then I got the phone call about Pop. Quitting seemed like the right thing at the time."

"I can only imagine. How've you been with it all? You went back to run his business, right?"

"It's all right. Some days it hits me all over again, but other days it's a bittersweet ache. And yeah, I'm running the store and added rental properties to the list."

"Wow. Do you ever talk to Alicia? I'd assumed you broke all ties..."

"We haven't talked since I left. I don't miss her at all." Now only Vivian filled his thoughts. And those thoughts had taken a downward turn. Michael cleared his throat. "You didn't say how you found out about her."

"She did the same thing to Ricardo."

Michael shook his head. That woman was poison.

"He came to my office with proof that she'd stolen his work. I then called her in and confronted her. She thought I was referring to you. When I mentioned Ricardo, the jig was up."

"Wow, Grady."

"Tell me about it. So, when are you coming back? We miss you."

It was nice to be needed, but Willow Springs was his home now. "I'm not."

Grady sighed. "It was worth a try. Though I still can't believe you live in a town small enough for only a general store."

"Willow Springs is perfect as it is. Maybe one day you'll visit and see why everyone loves it."

"Stranger things have happened."

They said their goodbyes, and Michael hung up. Relief warred with heartache as Michael thanked God that Alicia had been found out. When the dust had settled from Tropical Storm Alicia, Michael had easily been able to admit that he'd wanted out of the relationship for a while. Too bad his feelings over Vivian weren't so easily resolved. Knowing she'd kept secret something so vital tore him apart. He didn't want this to be the end of their friendship—or possibly more—but he couldn't see how he could ever trust her again. Not with all the omissions and evasions she'd tossed his way.

Was I really so wrong about her character, Lord? Why can't I meet a woman who has an impeccable character?

Vivian loved the Lord. Surely she couldn't have been lying about that. Everything out of her mouth had seemed genuine. Never gave him pause unless it was his own convictions he wrestled with. Had she been telling the truth about being worried over how he'd react?

She wasn't wrong, was she?

He winced. Maybe not, but how could he be with an alcoholic when his own father had perished at the hands of a drunk driver? That was more irony than he could handle. But a piece of him wouldn't let him forget the regret on Vivian's face or the fact that she'd tried to apologize.

Maybe he should have listened, but the pain stabbing his heart repeatedly told him to steer clear and leave womankind alone. He'd be a lot safer for it. Maybe this was the sign he needed that a relationship wasn't the best thing. He'd do better to eat, work and repeat—and leave Vivian out of the equation.

Chapter Sixteen

The next day, Vivian drove to work thinking about the day before. How sweet Ms. Ann had been to help her gain another perspective about the people who walked through the church's doors. They were believers because they'd experienced the grace of God—not because they were perfect beings who never messed up.

She had to remember that when the hurt of being ignored threatened to overwhelm her. Michael had ignored every attempt she'd made to talk with him. She'd finally set her phone down and prayed for the Lord to work in his heart. She didn't want to lose hope that they could mend their friendship, not like she'd lost hope of any reconciliation with her parents.

Focus on now. With a nod, Vivian walked into the church foyer. She frowned at raised voices coming from the sanctuary. No one had been scheduled to use the room for a meeting, and that certainly wasn't the praise team practicing. She pushed the double doors open and halted at the sight before her.

Indecipherable graffiti littered the back wall—a sight as horrifying as the liquor bottles strewn down the aisle.

"What in the world happened here?" She gasped.

The pastor looked up, and Ms. Ann hurried down the aisle toward her. "Someone came in sometime during the night and vandalized the place." She shook her head, black bob swaying. "Sheriff is on the way. We're just dumbfounded. Nothing like this happens in Willow Springs."

"Was anything stolen?" Vivian asked. She hugged Ms. Ann, then they linked arms as they walked back toward the pastor and the janitor.

"No. Pastor says everything is accounted for."

Mr. Prince squinted his eyes at her and thrust his broom handle in Vivian's face. "She probably did it. I heard her talking about being an alcoholic."

"Is that true?"

Vivian gasped at the sound of Michael's voice. She turned to see a look of consternation furrowing his brow. "Is what true?"

"Did you get drunk and vandalize the church?"

She reared back as if she'd been slapped.

"Michael Wood." Ms. Ann placed her hands on her hips. "I cannot believe you just accused Vivian of such a thing. Don't you know better?"

"She *is* an alcoholic, Ms. Ann." Michael's gaze met Vivian's, then zipped back to Ms. Ann's. "I don't know if she told you."

"She did, in her time. And so what if she hadn't? It's *not* my business." She turned to the janitor. "And how dare you make an accusation like that. Were you listening outside our door when we had that very *private* conversation, Mr. Prince?"

Vivian folded her arms around her waist. "Ms. Ann, please stop." Right now would be the perfect opportunity for a sinkhole to open up beneath her.

"I will not. They're maligning your character, and I

won't stand for it in a church, nor anywhere else I may draw breath. If everyone focuses on the *wrong* person," she shouted at the janitor, "then the police will waste their time instead of finding out who the real culprits are."

Vivian's head hurt. She'd thought today would be better than the day before. She wiped discreetly at the tears making their way down her face. "I think I should just go, Pastor," she said softly.

"It might be best. Just for today," he responded.

She nodded and headed up the aisle without a backward glance. She didn't slow when Ms. Ann called for her to wait, nor when she neared Michael. He sidestepped her, and she squeezed her eyes tight before opening them once more. She refused to break down any more than she already had. Well, at least in front of him. If the tears still felt like coming by the time she was back home, maybe she'd give in to them.

And it was fast becoming apparent that she couldn't stay at Simplicity Rentals any longer. If the accusations regarding the vandalism got out, staying in Willow Springs probably wouldn't be an option, either. She couldn't stay amid stares and whispers. It would break her heart further to see the joy she'd experienced in this town dwindle to heartache.

Yet her eyes were strangely dry as she drove back up to the Wood family's land. She ignored the beeping from the text she was sure was from Ms. Ann. Instead, she sang a worship song under her breath, hoping that her mind and heart would really believe "It Is Well."

She got out of the car and walked past the general store, stopping a few feet in front of her house. A woman sat on a patio chair, looking like she'd been waiting a couple of minutes. "Mom?"

The woman looked up.

It *was* her. Vivian covered her mouth with her hands, and her mom raced forward. They collided, squeezing each other in the dearest hug Vivian had ever had. She tucked her head into her mother's shoulder, the tears coming fast and hard as sobs racked her body.

Through it all, Mom rocked her and murmured, "We're okay. We'll be just fine."

When Vivian's cries dissipated, she stepped away from her mom. "I didn't think you'd come."

"I wasn't going to." Her mom swallowed. "But I found myself driving here anyway." She gestured to the house. "Should we talk inside?"

Vivian nodded and led the way straight to the living room area. "Do you want something to drink?"

"No, I had a cup of coffee on the way up." Her mom handed Vivian a tissue. "Want to tell me what the tears are for? I doubt it's simply for me."

It could be. She hadn't realized how much her mom's absence had weighed on her. "It's you but also something else."

"I'm sorry, Vivian. I didn't mean to hurt you, but I just couldn't let you back into our lives to break our hearts once more." Her mother looked down. "Your dad came around first. Told me we should forgive and not miss an opportunity to see you turn your life around." She gulped. "I'm afraid I didn't want to hear it and told him not to contact you. Then I woke up today feeling like I had to see you. Had to tell you I'm so sorry for letting the silence go on so long."

"It's all right. I'm just glad you came. And I'm not saying it didn't hurt." Because, boy, when sobriety had her mind right, the pain of their silence was awful. "But I do understand why you didn't believe me."

Her mother reached for her hand. "I do now. As soon

as you said my name and I saw your precious face, it was evident you'd changed."

Vivian wanted to blubber again. "I'm still sober. I promise you."

"I believe you, but it sounds like someone else might not?" Her mother arched an eyebrow in question.

The words tumbled out of Vivian—explaining what had happened between her and Michael, the vandalism at the Springs, and the accusations that she might be the cause of the trouble. Before long, her mom wiped her face and soothed Vivian as moms did best.

"They'll come around. See for themselves how wrong they were. I know they haven't known you that long, but it's so obvious you aren't under the influence any longer."

"I just can't believe the things Michael said. I know not telling him about my past hurt him. That was a huge mistake on my part. But how could he believe I would ever do something like that? I love my job, and I love this town."

Her mother rubbed her head. "I'm sorry. But if you have to start over again, that's not necessarily a bad thing. You should know—you've done it once already."

"I do, but I…" But Willow Springs had felt more like home than Little Rock ever did. How could she leave? But how could she stay?

"You can come home with me. See your father. Give yourself time to regroup and think."

"I still have work, Mom. But thank you."

Her phone pinged another notification. Should she look at them? Maybe they were from someone at the church—or maybe Michael was finally responding to her texts. Even so, she couldn't bring herself to look and see if she'd been rejected once more or if an apology would come her way.

* * *

Michael couldn't get Vivian's haunted look out of his brain. It was like someone had used flash photography to etch it into the back of his eyelids or used permanent marker to write on the walls of his mind. But he couldn't—*wouldn't*—think about that now.

"Pastor Liam, you wanted to see me?" Michael stood in the office doorway, noting the visitor already in the office. The pastor had asked Michael to stick around a few minutes after the sheriff had left earlier.

Liam motioned him forward, a heavy sigh falling from his lips. "That did not go well."

Mr. Prince looked at the pastor with a chagrined expression. "Suppose I should have waited until I had all the facts before accusing Ms. Dupre."

"You think?" the pastor asked. He shook his head, his blue eyes landing on Michael.

He stepped back, swallowing around the lump in his throat.

"You have anything *you* want to say, Michael?"

"No, sir."

Pastor Liam folded his arms as if he could wait all day for Michael to admit his guilt, which had been eating at him since he'd seen her haunted look. "I'm sorry."

"As much as those words are needed, I'm pretty sure you just said them to the wrong person."

Except he and Vivian weren't talking. The pastor didn't look like he wanted to hear any excuses from Michael's mouth, so he clamped his lips shut.

"Vivian didn't deface the church. For you two to suggest such a thing to a member in our community, a member of our church family, was offensive. What you weren't aware of was that Sheriff Rawley told me about the break-in and vandalism last night."

Michael's gut dropped to his feet. *Last night?* Still…

Pastor Liam pointed at the janitor. "I called you in to find out what you could do about getting the spray paint off the walls. If we need to have a paint party before midweek service, let me know and I'll rustle up some bodies."

"Understood, Pastor." Mr. Prince stood. "I'll get on that now."

"And Mr. Wood…"

"Yes?" Michael cleared his throat.

"The sheriff said you had a bit of trouble at your rentals. Do you suppose the same party could be behind this?"

Michael stifled a groan. How had he forgotten all about those guests? He hadn't even made the correlation between the rambunctious young adults and this. "Anything's possible at this point."

Pastor Liam got up from his chair and stepped into the hall. "Walk with me, Michael."

He did as instructed, wondering if they were going to address the elephant in the room or something else.

"I'd gotten the impression that you and Ms. Dupre were friends."

Michael blew out a breath. "Yes." Which was why her hiding the truth hurt so much. After all, he'd shared about his issues with his family, and he'd thought she'd been honest about hers. To find out she'd been holding back was a blow.

"I'm surprised, then, that you spoke to her with such bitterness and anger."

His jaw clenched. "I'd recently discovered she'd been hiding her past. That she's an alcoholic."

"Hmm. I suppose you thought she should have shared something like that with you?"

If they were really friends, wouldn't she have? "Like you said, I thought we were friends. Friends share that kind of stuff."

"Hmm. Then I imagine you've told her about Alicia?"

Michael stopped. "That's not the same thing. We aren't dating. I mean..." He'd wanted to but hadn't yet asked her out.

"And yet you want her to be open and vulnerable when you've held back yourself?"

"I..." His jaw worked. "She lied."

"So, you asked her if she was an alcoholic? She said no?"

"I didn't ask."

"I see." Pastor Liam stared right into his soul. "Do you suppose your hurt stems from the grief around how your father died and not necessarily the fact that Vivian hasn't shared everything she's been through?"

Michael squeezed his eyes shut. "I don't know." Because knowing she was an alcoholic, and adding the fact that a drunk driver had killed his dad, had jumbled all his thoughts like riding the Scrambler at the county fair.

"I think you need to work on forgiveness, and perhaps before you cast judgment, listen first. Before you open your mouth, have the whole story. You were out of line with Vivian. This is a house of God. We don't pass judgment against anyone who walks in here."

Shame heated the back of his neck, and it was all he could do to hold the pastor's gaze. "Yes, sir."

Pastor Liam clapped him on the back. "I do hope you'll mend fences."

"Have a good day, Pastor."

"You as well, Michael."

Michael walked through the double doors, struggling for composure. He'd come here to see if hospitality needed any refills on coffee or other drinks. Instead the pastor believed Michael needed to be pulled aside and dressed down.

Why did he have these feelings of guilt? He wasn't the one who had lied by omission. Vivian had. And no, he hadn't shared every single bit of information about himself with her, but they hadn't even known each other a full month.

Which scores points for the pastor questioning your reaction to her secret.

Michael rubbed a hand down his face and headed for his truck. Today had started off with him feeling like he'd been hit by a Mack truck and steadily gone downhill. Add the gutted feeling of Vivian's face haunting him, along with Pastor Liam's words, and Michael was ready to crawl back into bed and request a do-over.

Lord, why?

But like the fifty thousand other times he'd asked, silence greeted his ears. He swallowed as he drove back home. He pressed the phone icon on his navigation system and called Jordan.

"This is unexpected. Miss me already?"

"Vivian's an alcoholic."

"What!"

He winced at the volume in her voice—or maybe he just needed to turn the car audio down.

"When did she tell you?"

"She didn't." And the thought burned.

"How did you find out then?"

"I saw her breathe into those things they put on your steering wheel after you get DWIs."

"Seriously? Did she have an explanation?"

He rubbed his beard. "I…may have not been ready to listen."

"Oh, brother. Sounds like you need a Wood family meeting. I'll text the others and we'll FaceTime later. 'Kay?"

"Yeah. I suppose."

"I know after Alicia this probably came as a shock, but don't jump to conclusions."

"That may already be too late."

"Were you mean?"

Was he? He winced. *Uh.* "I might have been."

"Okay. I'll tell the others we need to FaceTime ASAP. What are you doing now?"

"Driving back home. The church was vandalized, and Pastor Liam wondered if anyone renting at Simplicity could have been the culprit."

"Such as Vivian?"

"I might have suggested her name."

Jordan gasped. "You didn't. You know what? Don't tell me any more. You'll just have to repeat it for everyone else anyway. Call you later."

He groaned. This was bad. No matter how he examined everything, it just seemed like it would all end badly. *Please, let me be wrong, Lord. Please.*

Chapter Seventeen

Vivian held the door open, letting her mom enter the Sassy Spoon first.

"It smells delicious in here," Mom said.

"I always get so hungry just walking in." Vivian pointed to the side of the room with booths. "Want to sit over there?"

"Sure. Lead the way."

Vivian walked forward and almost tripped as some of the diner patrons looked at her then away. Some even began whispering to their tablemates. *What's going on?*

She swallowed as she sank into the booth cushion, her mom sliding across the leather to sit across from her.

"Is it me or are they talking about us?" Mom whispered, leaning forward.

"I thought something similar. Pretty sure they're talking about me. You don't think..." Her voice trailed off.

Movies always portrayed small towns as gossip spreaders, but Vivian had never experienced that in Willow Springs. Until now.

"Maybe we should eat somewhere else, Mom?" *Like home.* Though who knew where that would be after New Year's. Her mom's offer echoed in Vivian's mind. Could

Little Rock be home once more, or should she tough it out in Willow Springs?

"We'll do no such thing. You have nothing to be ashamed of." Mom lifted her chin in that stubborn tilt she often used when deciding to stick to her beliefs.

"I don't know, Mom." Vivian wanted to disappear. It was like everyone knew her secret and judged her for it. Did they know she'd been in jail, too? She gasped.

"What is it?" Mom reached for Vivian's hand.

"We need to go."

"Are you sure?"

She nodded. Because the thought of Michael finding out about her incarceration from someone other than herself made her want to reach for the nearest wastebasket and lose her breakfast.

You didn't eat this morning, remember?

"All right. Tell me what's wrong in the car."

Vivian said nothing, simply leaned on her mom as they walked back outside and to Mom's luxury sedan. Thankfully, she'd spared Vivian from blowing into that stupid breathalyzer.

"What happened back there?"

"Michael doesn't know I was in jail." Her breath came in spurts, and panic clawed up her throat. "And I don't know if those whispers back there were about that or my alcoholism or the church damage."

"Oh, dear."

"Right?" she cried.

She dropped her head in her hands as she tried to pull some spiritual truth to the forefront of her mind. But everything was blank. She remained silent the entire car ride back. As soon as her mom turned into the general store's parking lot, Vivian asked her to stop.

She slipped her key ring out of her purse. "Just wait

for me at the tiny house. I'll cook us up something when I get back."

"Or I can putter around while you have your talk." Her mom's brow furrowed with concern.

"Thanks, Mom." Vivian slid an arm around her shoulders. Amazing how God knew when she'd need the comfort of her mother.

"Anytime."

Vivian said a prayer as she walked up the front steps to the store. Hopefully no one was shopping right now. Alas, four heads swiveled in her direction when she entered the store. Michael stood behind the counter, ringing up Ms. Ann. Two other patrons quickly averted their gazes when Vivian spared them a glance. *Great, they're hearing rumors, too.*

Her face heated as she headed for Ms. Ann and Michael.

"Hello, dear. How are you?"

Vivian shrugged. "Time will tell."

"That's the God's honest truth." She turned back to Michael. "Thank you. See you Wednesday."

"'Bye, Ms. Ann."

Vivian stepped forward, gripping the counter. "Is there any possible way I can talk to you upstairs for a brief moment?"

His eyes widened, and his gaze flickered behind her.

"Please? I *have* to tell you something."

"Fine." In a louder voice, he spoke to the patrons. "Be right back, folks. Forgot something upstairs."

"Take your time, Big Mike."

Michael motioned for her to go first. She trod up the stairs, nerves doing acrobatics in her middle. What would he say? Would he hate her even more than he already did? Would he make her move out right this moment? As soon as the door closed behind her, perspiration beaded across her forehead. She licked her lips and turned.

"I didn't have a chance to tell you everything, and judging from some stares in town, rumors might be going around. I wanted to come clean to you before someone else could tell you something first, or worse, spread lies."

"You're making me nervous, Vivian."

"I'm sorry. I'm so, so sorry." She blinked against the tears, willing them to stay away until she could be alone—well, just her and her mom. She needed to get this out quickly.

"You've already said that."

"Yes. But you need to know I'm sorry you got blind-sided. Sorry I didn't trust you with my story. Plus, I'm very sorry for what I'm about to tell you." She drew in a breath. *Lord, please give me the words.* "That interlock ignition device isn't the whole story."

Michael folded his arms. "Go on."

"About seven months ago, I was sentenced to serve six months in county jail. Though it was my first offense of driving while intoxicated, the fact that I ran into a police cruiser had the judge adding jail time." Vivian couldn't look him in the eye and see the disgust there.

She swallowed and continued. "Before then, I was an alcoholic who wouldn't admit I needed help. Once I was in jail and forced to become sober, I quickly real-ized how much help I truly needed. It was in a weekly church service hosted by a local pastor that I found Jesus, and not some ploy to get off for good behavior or any-thing like that." She pointed to her heart. "I mean I *hon-estly* found Jesus. He cleaned me up, gave me a second chance here in Willow Springs and has loved me through all my mess-ups."

And wow, how she wanted to ask if it were possible

Michael could love her through her mistakes as well. But what right did she have? They'd never declared any feelings past friendship. Not to mention the huge issue that stood before them now—her past.

"I'm so sorry I hurt you and didn't tell you," she ended on a whisper.

The room stood silent—too silent. Fear had glued her eyes to her feet as she waited for Michael to say something.

"Now that you've told me, you can leave. I have work to do."

She covered the sob rising up her throat. She didn't argue, just headed for the door as tears begged to be released behind her hot eyelids.

The whole way down the stairs, all she could do was ask the Lord to get her through one more mess-up. She kept her eyes on the ground, taking it one step at a time to put some distance between herself and Michael and the townspeople who were eager to hear whatever she had to share.

As soon as she rounded the house outside, her cries erupted and she ran all the way to her tiny home and into the safety of her mother's arms.

He had absolutely no words. Michael stood there, staring at the place Vivian had just vacated, searching for any piece of comprehension. He gulped, his face feeling hot, but he wasn't sure why. Was he going to be sick to his stomach? Was it shame on her behalf?

When his pocket buzzed, he pulled out his cell phone and answered the video call.

"Whoa, Michael, you look *awful*," Pippen said.

"For real," Chuck chimed in.

"Y'all give him an opportunity to talk and you'll find out why," Jordan stated.

Michael sank to the sofa. "I'm speechless. I can't..." He shook his head.

"You sure had a lot of things to say earlier," Jordan said.

"Yeah, well, you have a lot to say when you're trying to make sense of some new information." He rubbed his jaw. "Vivian just stopped by with a bigger bombshell than the last."

"The last?" Pippen asked.

"Yes, can someone catch me up?" Chuck raised his hand.

"Can I?" Jordan asked.

"Please." Michael wasn't sure how he would even tell them about Vivian serving six months in jail.

He half listened as Jordan shared about Vivian being an alcoholic and his not-so-bright reaction to the news.

"So is she sober now?" Chuck asked. "She doesn't sound like she's drunk whenever I see her."

"She says she is." Michael blew out a breath.

"Is that what she stopped by to talk about? An explanation for why she didn't say anything before?" Jordan asked.

He shook his head and rubbed his eyes. "She, uh, she apparently served time for her DWI." He swallowed. "Six months in county jail. Said that's where she sobered up and found Jesus." He stared at the video on his phone to witness varying degrees of shock on his siblings' faces.

"Uh," Pippen stuttered.

Jordan waved a hand. "Hold up. Hold up. *Hold up!* Jail? For real?"

"I wouldn't joke about something like that." He needed a bottle of antacids to get through reality right now.

"I'd rather you prank us than this be the truth." Shock covered Chuck's features.

"This is why I don't like church." Pippen rolled her eyes. "So many hypocritical people in there."

Now Michael's mouth dropped. Since when did Pip feel that way? "Are you serious?"

"As serious as your convict. She's been walking around like she's Miss Pure and she's breathing into a breathalyzer."

"But Pip, no one ever claimed that church is filled with perfect people who've never sinned. The church is full of *forgiven* sinners." Chuck shook his head. "I'm frankly surprised you're so upset about this, Mike. I thought you liked Viv."

"I did." *Still do.* "That's why this is such a shock. In all the time we've hung out, she's never shared or even hinted at a secret this huge." Though hadn't he been wary? At the time, he chalked the feelings up to his troubled history with Alicia.

"Maybe this is why." Jordan wagged a finger. "People like Pip acting scandalized. Even yourself, *brother* dear. She probably felt like she had to walk on eggshells so people wouldn't clutch their pearls or judge her."

"We don't do that at church. Anyone is welcome." Yet he barely hid a wince as he remembered the dressing-down Pastor Liam had given him for his own judgmental reaction.

Pip snorted. "Obviously."

"Enough, Pippen," Chuck snapped. "I'd like to see you go through something like that and bounce back with the amount of grace and kindness Vivian has shown."

Shouldn't that be him defending her? And yeah, Pippen's comments were getting under Michael's skin, but he also understood the shock. Vivian had presented herself as blameless to the people of the Springs Bible Church.

But didn't being forgiven by Jesus gain her that right? He rubbed his face. "I don't know what to do. What to think."

"Did you pray?" Chuck asked.

"Yes. Though more of a whine than an actual *help me*–type prayer."

"Then go take a hike and pray. That always clears your head," Jordan suggested.

He nodded. He hadn't been hiking in a while. "I don't know if I have the time. It's been really busy around here."

"How busy?" Pippen asked.

He relayed all the things he had to do. "And that's only for today."

Raised eyebrows went up on all his siblings' faces.

"Do you need help there?" Jordan asked.

Michael swallowed. Now was the time to be real. "Yes. I might even finally have the funds to pay someone a salary."

She bit her lip. "How about instead of a full salary, you offer me room and board?"

He sat forward. "Then you're coming back home?" Did this mean the roommate situation had tanked?

"If that's okay with you."

"More than okay. I'd love the help and company."

Jordan grinned. "Great. I'll take Pip's and my old room. If that's okay with you."

"Of course."

"Then I'll be there in about two weeks. Once I give notice at work."

"Great." Before they hung up, Michael brought up

the pastor's insinuation that anger about Pop's death had clouded his vision.

Silence greeted him.

"Y'all think he's right, don't you?"

"It's something to think about," Chuck said. He frowned and looked down. "Hey, I'm getting paged for work. Talk to y'all later."

His square disappeared off the phone, then Pip said goodbye. Michael looked at Jordan.

"What are you thinking, Jay?"

"That you should really examine yourself and ask how Jesus would treat Vivian. Then apologize profusely for acting like a Pharisee and ask for her forgiveness."

His insides twisted. From the moment he discovered Vivian's secret, he'd been acting like the injured party. But being compared to a Pharisee did something to his insides. "Ugh," he groaned, dropping his head in his hands. "She must hate me."

"Grovel," Jordan added.

"All right."

He hung up, then sat back to do an honest self-reflection. Because if he'd been the kind of guy that Christ had called *hypocrite* more than once in the Bible, then Michael needed a serious heart check.

Chapter Eighteen

The tiny home looked bare, since Vivian had packed away most of the possessions she'd slowly begun to accrue. All she needed to do was give her notice to the church and pray they could find a new secretary so that the Ms. Ann would still be able to move and be with her family.

Granted, Vivian wasn't planning on leaving town on Christmas Eve, like her mom had suggested. Michael had given her until the new year, so she'd hold him to that. It would give her time to find a job in Little Rock and a new place to live. She'd miss Willow Springs, that's for sure.

She swallowed, grabbed her purse and headed for the door. Her plan upon waking this morning was to talk to Pastor Liam and give her notice. Yet the thought had her stomach twisting and her mind shouting denials. Should she consider staying in Willow Springs? Keeping her job? No way. She'd have to endure the looks of condemnation and scorn if she remained.

Still, the questions repeated themselves all through her drive to the church parking lot. After climbing from her car, she shut the door, but before she could take a step, someone shouted her name. Vivian whirled around and found Cecelia and Yvonne waving across the street. She returned the gesture, a little stunned they were trying to get her attention. They had to be a few of the people in Willow Springs that actually wanted to speak to her.

The women crossed the street, stopping in front of Vivian before she could wrap her mind around this turn of events.

"Hey," Cecelia said softly.

"Hi." Vivian swallowed and looked at the ladies. "I take it you've heard?"

"We've heard lots of things." Yvonne placed a hand on her hip. "What we want to know is what's actually true, so we decided to hear it from the source—*you*."

Tears sprang to her eyes. They wanted to hear what she had to say? "Um. I was about to go inside. Want to come in?"

"We'll follow. I'm sure Ms. Ann won't mind," Yvonne said.

They walked quietly into the office, and Vivian let out a sigh when she saw Ms. Ann's empty seat. She gestured for the women to pull up some chairs.

"So, what have you heard?" Why she led with that, she had no idea. Maybe out of curiosity to know what the townspeople thought?

Yvonne waved a hand in the air. "Let's skip gossip and get down to facts."

"I can do that." Vivian swallowed. "I'm an alcoholic and have been sober for almost seven months."

"Good for you." Cecelia smiled. "I'm sure that was hard to do."

Her eyes watered. Were they really going to be this understanding? "It was." She swallowed. "But it got easier when I accepted Christ as my savior." She licked her lips. "Soon I filled my empty time with reading the Bible to learn all I could about Him and make a permanent change in my life."

"It sounds like that's what you've done," Yvonne said. "I mean, you are secretary here. You never miss a Wednesday or Sunday service."

"I don't. I read my Bible every day to make sure I start my morning centered on Him." Here went the hard part—going deeper into her past than just the drinking problem. "That's not all. I also served six months in jail for a DWI. And because of that, I have an interlock ignition device on my vehicle for another five months. The jail time plus probation time—if I adhere to all the rules—will allow me to have the charge expunged from my record."

"Oh, good." Cecelia breathed a sigh of relief. "You never know with something like that."

"Really? You've had experience with people in jail?"

Cecelia nodded. "My father served time for burglary. It was hard, because people looked at me like I would do the same thing. So, I get what it's like for rumors to swirl around you."

Yvonne made a sound of agreement. "Willow Springs is a good town, but we do have our gossips. For the most part, people don't throw stones. How can we when we all have a skeleton or two we'd like to stay buried?"

"Then you guys still want to be my friends?" Could this really be happening?

"Of course we do." Cecelia reached across the table and squeezed Vivian's hand. "We're friends now, Viv. Don't let this little hiccup set you back."

Should she tell them about moving back to Little Rock? She glanced at the clock and determined there was enough time before she had to start work. "I packed my stuff. Well, not all of it. I needed clothes to wear and whatnot, but I'm planning on moving back to Little Rock."

"Why?" Yvonne cried. "Over some paltry rumors?"

"I don't want people to stare at me accusingly or with criticism." Vivian gripped the edge of the desk. "I don't think I could stand under the pressure for too long."

"What kind of accusations have you received?" Cecelia asked.

She sighed. "Did you hear about the vandalism?"

"Wait," Yvonne gasped. "That rumor is true? People think you really did that?"

Vivian nodded. "Judging by the stares and the one person I thought I could trust suggesting so, yes."

"What? Michael accused you?" Cecelia gaped.

Vivian wanted to groan and bang her head against the desk. Anything but relive the hurt that had shafted through her insides at the pain etched into his features. "Part of the reason I'm planning to move."

"But, Viv, you just can't," Cecelia pleaded.

"Have you prayed about this?" Yvonne's gaze assessed her.

Vivian shifted in her seat. "Well, not in an *ask for guidance* kind of way. More of a *what now* and *please help me.* I do need to find a job and a place to live back in Little Rock."

"Sounds like you need to back up a few steps."

But she didn't want to. All she wanted was a nice place to hide and lick her wounds. *Ugh.* That so wasn't what God wanted for her, but… "I don't know, you guys. I can't see how dealing with rumors is part of living abundantly."

"What are you afraid of?"

"That God will ask me to stay and face these judgmental people." Because some days, Vivian couldn't even face herself.

"Vivian..."

She jumped, turning to stare at the doorway.

"Could I speak with you?" Pastor Liam asked.

"We were just leaving, Pastor." Cecelia stood abruptly, then glanced at Vivian. "Talk to you later."

"Remember what I said," Yvonne whispered, then followed behind the other woman.

"Should I come into your office?" Vivian asked. "Or would you like to sit?"

And where was Ms. Ann? Was she sick? Too ashamed to sit in the same office as Vivian? No, of course not. She'd been kind to Vivian this entire time.

"Yes. I won't be long." He sat across from her. "Ms. Ann came down with a stomach bug but assured me you could handle everything on your own."

She nodded. *Please heal Ms. Ann.* "I can. I'm sorry she's sick."

"Yeah, something's going around town."

"Was that all you wanted to talk about?" Or were they going to address her sinking reputation?

He tilted his head. "I couldn't help but hear the tail end of your conversation. I apologize for overhearing, but I just wanted to talk about what I heard. Are you really thinking of leaving town?"

"Yes. I've already packed the majority of my stuff."

He rubbed his chin. "Will you stay at least until the end of the year?"

"That's what I was going to talk to you about. I wanted to give my two weeks' notice."

"I wish you'd reconsider. We value your work and your friendship."

She squeezed her hands together, glad the desk hid her movements.

"And if you haven't prayed about it, as one of your

friends hinted at, I'd like to give you food for thought and a reason to pray."

"All right," she drew out.

"Have you read the chapter in the Bible where Jesus meets the Samaritan women at the well?"

Vivian sat up. She actually had, though she hadn't really understood the significance until she'd done a little research. Apparently, the Jews and Samaritans hadn't gotten along. "I have."

"What's the one thing that stuck out to you?"

"That Jesus offered her living water." Vivian had clung to that while serving her time, in those moments when staying sober and not thinking of her next drink seemed impossible. "Is that what sticks out with you?"

"Each time I read it, I notice a little detail I haven't before. It's one of my favorite things about reading the Bible." Pastor Liam smiled. "I feel that the Lord meets us with a new nugget when we need it. It's why I want to share what stayed with me the last time I read it."

"I'm listening."

"The woman didn't let the weight of her past prevent her from going out to the people and telling them about how she'd met the Messiah."

Vivian blinked, heart pounding.

Pastor Liam stood and offered a soft smile. "Remember that, Vivian, and remember we all have a past. Perhaps you should pray and ask the Lord how He wants you to use it."

"I will," she whispered. Because left with that wisdom, how could she not?

"Good. I'll talk to you later."

Michael dragged in a deep inhale of the crisp winter air. The Lost Valley trail was one of the most popular hiking trails in Arkansas. Right now, the frozen scenery gave the trail a majestic feel. As if nature had thrown out all the pomp and circumstance for hikers. He strolled down the rocky path past a bluff. Should he take a breather and sit on a log to admire God's creation or continue on until he came to his favorite waterfall? The soothing noise of the water always managed to relax him and help clear his mind.

Decision made, he strode up the hill, passing icicled tree branches. His steps began to slow as the sound of water trickled to his ears. Taking the path that led to Eden Falls, Michael came to a stop and smiled. Part of the waterfall had frozen, creating hanging ice sculptures off the rocky cave.

"God, are You with me?" He spoke softly, because something about this spot had him wanting to honor God's creation and not spook any animals that could wander by. The Ponca area had been known to have elk, but he couldn't recall if they ever came this way. They were his favorite and made him think of the Lord for some reason. Not that they were the only creatures in the area he didn't want to scare, just his favorite.

He found a spot to sit and took off his hiking pack, placing it to his right. Last night hadn't provided him with a good night's rest. He'd tossed through the hours thinking of the past two days and all his emotions surrounding the events.

When he woke this morning, more angst greeted him. Or, as Jordan used to say, his brood mode had been activated. He ran a hand down his face, staring at the water. He couldn't think any more because his mind kept stopping at the fact that Vivian had had every opportunity to tell him about her past, and she hadn't. After all they'd shared, all the vulnerability—that he'd assumed was on both their parts—she kept that a secret. Hadn't volunteered the information when she found out about Pop—

Okay, something like that would've given him pause if the shoe was on the other foot. In fact, maybe he needed to stop looking at it from his own standpoint. Because obviously he would continuously come to the same conclusion. What he needed to do was put himself in her shoes and think about what her world was like.

To be locked up for six months, sober up, meet Jesus—which he did actually believe was real. Unlike Pippen, he didn't believe the church was full of hypocrites but hurting people who had found the healer. So, if Vivian's conversion was real, then how would that impact how she handled her past?

Neither do I condemn thee.

He swallowed, remembering the words of the Bible. Jesus would've forgiven Vivian and opened His arms wide for her return to the fold. If Jesus's followers—aka Michael—were supposed to imitate His behavior, then Michael had failed grossly. He'd tossed accusations, demanded she leave—

His stomach dropped to his toes, and he fell to his knees. "Lord, what have I done? How did I let anger get the best of me?" Or, as Pastor Liam suggested, let grief twist his heart into unforgiveness.

Because if he forgave Vivian, he'd have to forgive the driver who killed Pop.

The sound of trickling water filled his ears, reminding him of where he was and why he'd stopped at Eden Falls. Aptly named, considering he wanted to feel closer to God, to be able to hear His still, small voice.

"I'm so sorry, Lord. Sorry I failed. Sorry I didn't welcome her with open arms." Because before that little bomb dropped, he'd been thinking of dating her, of having a future together.

With one little discovery, Michael had backtracked so fast, he'd gotten tire marks on his own body. Was there a way to repair the damage his hasty words had caused? If Michael had been in the same position, he knew without a doubt, he'd want to be welcomed by church members and the community at large. He'd want a new beginning and for his past not to be an albatross.

Wasn't that the message Vivian had tried to convey to him? He'd been too stubborn to hear her out and actually *listen* to what she told him. All he could think about was the hurt *he* was in, instead of considering someone else's needs before his own.

He groaned. He. Was. The. Worst.

Lord, please forgive me for how I treated Vivian. Please help me forgive the man who killed Pop. Please heal the unforgiveness and anger in my heart.

Maybe Vivian would be willing to forgive him and take a chance on him. Michael stood and reached for his hiking pack, swinging it over his shoulder. He drew in a deep breath.

Lord, is there any way You could pave a way for me? Could Vivian truly forgive me?

He swallowed, knowing what the rest of his prayer needed to reflect.

Not for my sake, though I want that, too, Lord. But I don't want my judgmental attitude to cause her harm or have her leaving the church. I also pray that Pastor Liam and Sheriff Rawley find the real culprit of the vandalism. And please, may Vivian be willing to give me another chance. A real *chance. Amen.*

Michael turned away from the falls and headed back to the main trail, then started hiking to where he'd parked.

Hopefully Vivian would be around when he returned to Simplicity. He needed to talk and apologize for being the biggest fool in Willow Springs. If she was gone, then maybe he'd rely on his cell—not to text his apologies, but to request a meeting instead. No way he would beg forgiveness without being face-to-face.

His breath caught. Right before him stood an elk, its antlers grandiose. Michael smiled and looked up between the leaves to the sky. *Thank You.*

Chapter Nineteen

She didn't know what to do.

Was packing up and moving out of Willow Springs a hasty decision? Vivian loved this area. The kindness she'd experienced from the townspeople when she'd first arrived. The way they decorated for the holidays. Not to mention how participating in the Christmas Wishes ministry had grounded her in a way she hadn't even known was possible. Giving to others had allowed her to not wallow in her own problems but focus on lifting another's spirits in the midst of their trials. Not only that, but she knew for a fact those families felt blessed by the community.

Willow Springs had offered her so much. How could she just abandon them?

"Lord, what do I do?"

The question was on instant replay and had become its own prayer. Yet for all the time she prayed, Vivian couldn't discern an answer. Was she not asking the right question? Was she not devoting enough quiet time to be still and determine the Lord's direction?

When Yvonne had asked if Vivian had prayed, she

hadn't known what to tell her. Because her prayers had all seemed surface level—mere petitions to get her out of the situation instead of asking how He wanted her to proceed.

She set her mug on the coffee table and curled her legs underneath her. Leaning back against the sofa cushion, she breathed in deeply and slowly let out the exhale. Clearing her mind was something she'd learned to help push out the urges of wanting a drink. When she committed her life to Christ, she'd added praying to her mindfulness routine. Now she opened up her heart, pouring out all the hurts she'd endured, the mistake of not telling Michael sooner and the question of where to call home.

She even let the Lord know just how hurt she was by the accusations Michael had spewed at her, not to mention Mr. Prince and the gossiping townspeople. They'd all contributed to fracturing her perception of Willow Springs—even validated her reasoning behind keeping her past a secret. Though her guilt about not telling Michael still weighed on her.

It was so easy to focus on her hurt and the shame she felt when people's gazes drifted away from her, hoping she'd get the idea by the lack of eye contact. She could claim to be the injured party, the victim in the townspeople's wrath and need for a culprit for the church vandalism. But was that the whole truth?

She'd easily shifted to that place of hurt instead of what had started it all—her need to shelter her past and feel safe instead of coming clean the moment Michael started opening up to her as a trusted source. A person who would willingly listen to his problems. In that vulnerable state, she should have trusted him in return. Instead, she'd assumed he'd think the worst of her, and she'd lose his esteem and continue her life as a pariah.

Vivian glanced at the cardboard boxes near the front door. If anyone had treated her like an exile, it was her own reaction. She'd jumped the gun and decided to remove herself from the situation. Yes, Michael had asked her to move out, but even she could tell that had been out of hurt. Granted, rentals in Willow Springs were practically nonexistent, so knowing her options was vital if she was going to continue to live here.

Despite her mother's suggestion of moving back to Little Rock, Vivian could now admit that was a knee-jerk reaction. She'd been too hasty in packing. Willow Springs was her home, and she needed to fight for it.

A knock sounded, and she jumped. No one ever visited her, and her mother had driven back to Little Rock yesterday evening. She opened the door and froze.

"Michael..."

His Adam's apple bobbed. "May I come in...please?"

She folded her arms. "If you need me to move out sooner, just tell me now."

"No!" He blanched. "I came here to apologize."

Vivian scoffed. She couldn't help it. He'd been so adamant about her guilt and now he wanted to apologize? She was supposed to believe he'd flipped a switch and suddenly felt repentant?

Isn't that how it happens for some people?

"I was way out of line and *never* should have passed judgment. I should have heard you out like you asked, but I let my emotions get the better of me."

Her breath stuttered. What could she say to that? She completely understood how he'd reacted. It was the one thing she'd feared the more she'd gotten to know him.

But the hurt he'd caused was still present. How could it not be the same way for him?

"How can I trust what you're saying? You were livid the other day. How can those feelings just be gone?" She whispered the last part.

"I don't expect you to accept everything I'm saying right now. If you need to pray about it—whatever you need, I'll wait. I..." He swallowed. "The way Pop died, I can see why that knowledge would make you guard your past. I didn't realize how much bitterness I had unresolved until..." He sighed, rubbing his beard. "What I'm trying to say is, I get it. I was awful, and I pray you can forgive me."

Her heart pounded as her mind dissected every word he said. "Is that all?" Not that she really expected him to say much else.

"Uh...actually, I have something else." He slid his hands into his pockets. "One of the reasons I reacted so badly was because I'd been hoping our friendship would lead to more. I'd gathered the courage to ask you out, then I saw you in your car." He winced. "If I could go back and change my reaction, I would. Please know I'm so very sorry."

Was he saying he had feelings for her? The kind that led to dating and long-lasting relationships? Her mind was a mess as she tried to weed through the new information and his apology. Should she give him grace?

Pray about it. That's what Michael had said and probably the first step she should take. "Okay." She licked her lips. "I'll pray."

He nodded slowly. "Thank you." He hitched a thumb over his shoulder. "Well, I gotta get back to work."

"Don't you have a lot going on?" Should she offer to assist him again? After all, he knew her secret this time.

"I do, but Jordan's moving back. She's going to help me out for room and board."

"Good. I hope that relieves your stress."

A longing look filled his eyes. "I'm so not good enough for you."

Vivian blinked. "Where did that come from?"

"I acted a fool, and here you stand hoping my stress goes away."

"Well, you were so worried—"

"I was." He shifted on his feet. "I am. I just, after everything that happened between us, didn't expect you to still care."

"I'm not a robot. I can't just turn off feelings like I would a faucet."

He stepped forward. "Does that mean you care? More than friendship dictates?"

She shouldn't. She hadn't been sober a year. But as Vivian stared into his eyes, saw the caring, the hope, she measured her own response. "I do, but I can't give you a yes right now. Not that you're asking anything."

"I am," he replied swiftly. "I'm asking if you want to be with me. If you want to be my girlfriend. I'm asking."

Vivian felt the urge to smile battle with the desire to not make the wrong move. "I don't know what to think."

"I get it." He gulped. "And you don't have to leave, Vivian." His gaze drifted to the floor, where the corner of a cardboard box peeked out. "Please don't," he said softly. "That was unprofessional, not to mention the opposite of how friends respond."

She wanted to sag against the door frame. Instead she nodded. "I'll talk to you later."

He mumbled his parting as she closed the door. She pressed her forehead to the wood and let the tears fall.

How could something like an apology and someone wanting to date her wreck her so thoroughly?

The yellow door stared at him as Michael stood debating what to do next. He said he'd give Vivian time, and he wholeheartedly meant that. But now what? There had to be something else he could do to show her he wouldn't desert her in her time of need. That he wouldn't open his mouth and shove the dirty size-thirteen boot into it.

He ran a hand over his beard and strolled away. His mind raced as he prayed, listened, prayed some more. Maybe there was nothing to do in this situation but wait. Maybe simply showing her he was a man of his word would be enough.

He also couldn't get that one verse out of his head about fruit worthy of repentance. What was his fruit? In his opinion, an apology was only a sprout.

As he neared the back of the house, loud music blared from one of the tiny homes. *Ugh.* Not those guys again. He pivoted on his heel and stalked toward the problem renters. It was time for them to go. He couldn't have them disturbing the peace for his other tenants or wreaking havoc throughout Willow Springs.

He pounded on the door, hoping the fist he made sounded loud enough to break through the music thumping the ground. The volume lowered, and the door opened.

One of the tenants smirked. "Let me guess, we're too loud?"

"Why state the obvious? I'd like you to examine the rental agreement you signed, then vacate immediately."

The guy blinked. "Are you serious? Bruh!"

Michael folded his arms. "I'm very serious. You're in violation of the tenant agreement, which means I have the right to ask you to leave." Could the man read the gravity of the situation or would he argue?

"Bruh. I can't believe this."

"Believe it."

"Then I want my money back."

"Again. Read the tenant agreement you *signed* and go. I don't owe you a single penny, and you may be charged a cleanup fee." Michael pointed to the garbage littering the floor then froze.

In the mix of the alcoholic beverages were spray-paint cans.

His gaze darted to the tenant, and the young man's eyes widened. He slammed the door shut before Michael could so much as dart a hand out. Instead, he pulled out his cell and called the sheriff's office.

"Is this an emergency or nonemergency situation?"

"Nonemergency, Darlene. Can you tell the sheriff I believe one of Simplicity's renters is responsible for the vandalism at the church? I was in the process of asking him to vacate when I spied some spray-paint cans."

"Hold on, Mike."

He rubbed the back of his neck while hold music tried to soothe him and assure him everything would work out. But all he felt was guilt for accusing Vivian, guilt for harboring a criminal—unintentionally didn't matter in his eyes—and guilt for not suspecting these guys sooner. Though after Pastor Liam brought it up, the sheriff had made every attempt to question them. They were never home though. Should have known because they'd been trouble from day one.

"Hey, Mike, Sheriff was on the road but will make a detour to your place. He said don't engage the suspect but please call back if they leave before he gets there."

"Understood."

"Have a good day."

"You, too, Darlene." He didn't understand why people went through the motions of pleasantry, but right now, he genuinely wished she had a better day than his.

Five minutes later, Rawley pulled into the parking lot. Michael stepped off the front porch of the general store to meet him.

"They haven't left." He pointed to a green cube-looking car. "That's their vehicle."

"All right. These the same guys who had the allergic reaction kid?"

"Right."

Rawley groused, "I know we rely on tourism, but I can't abide disrespectful folk. Ain't no reason to come up here and cause trouble. Getting outdoors is supposed to shake some sense into a man, not knock things loose."

Michael chuckled. "If it makes you feel better, I'm pretty sure they were missing common sense before they got here. Plus the compass to lead them to it."

"Nah, I don't feel better, just pity. Someone ought to teach them better."

"Guess that's why you're here, Sheriff." Michael clapped him on the back and pointed out the house they were in. "That one right there. Should I go inside?"

"Yep. No need to cause a scene. I've got your cell if I have any follow-up questions."

"Thanks." Michael swallowed. "Can I tell Vivian?"

"Don't jump the gun. There's a process, and right now, you just have rowdy tenants and spray cans. Not enough to connect the dots yet."

He sighed. "Very well. Keep me posted, please."

"Of course, Big Mike. Thanks for looking out."

Michael nodded, then headed back inside. He needed to open the store back up now that his lunch hour was over. Though a quick glance at his watch told him he could spare a few minutes to think about all that had transpired.

Lord, please, let them be the guys. Clear Vivian's name and heal the hurt we've caused.

He knew he'd played a big part in her wounds, but the town gossips just twisted the knife a little too far. Willow Springs was better than that, and Michael had to find a way to show Vivian.

Chapter Twenty

The clouds covered the night sky, and Vivian shivered underneath a blanket as she sat on the makeshift porch in front of her rental. A lot had happened in the past few days that had left her head spinning like a fidget toy. Now that life had stopped throwing surprises her way, she'd been able to slow down enough to examine all the events.

What she found didn't give her any warm fuzzies.

She'd been so ready to flee, to run away from her problems. She'd thought becoming a Christian and sobering up would erase some of her old patterns. Yet when faced with opposition and accusations, she'd curled up like a roly-poly, ready to play dead. Then when her mom had made the offer to return to Little Rock, she'd taken it as a sign that her fresh start had failed and so had she.

But after talking with her friends and the pastor and receiving Michael's apologies, Vivian had taken a hard look at herself. She wanted to be like the woman at the well, proud to tell the world what Jesus had done and would continue doing for her. What He could do for others, and what He would do for them in the future. She didn't want to curl up in a defensive posture and retreat to safety. After all, the Israelites had thought going back to Egypt better than what lay in the wilderness, and that hadn't turned out well for them.

No, Vivian needed to put her faith into action and trust where God had led her and what He had in store in this little town that had stolen her heart. She breathed in, and a soft smile crossed her lips. Staying was the right thing to do. It was where God had planted her and where she wanted to flourish.

Lord, please give me courage to face mountains and feet like deer to climb them. Amen.

Now came the question of what to do with Michael. Knowing he wanted to date her sent a thrill right through her. But Kate had cautioned her about jumping into a romantic relationship before being a year sober. And seven months was no year.

And she couldn't help but believe that God was okay with their relationship. So what did that mean? She hadn't realized how gun-shy she really was about dating until Michael told her his thoughts.

Lord, what do I tell him? Is there a way to say yes but not yet? But she didn't want to toy with him. Nothing that would make him think she couldn't be open and honest. Before she could think any further, footfalls reached her ears. She turned, and her breath stuttered at the sight before her.

Michael had on a sheepskin jacket, jeans and a red beanie. "Hey."

"Hi." She stood. What was he doing out here? Had the general store already closed?

"Are you busy?"

"No. I was thinking the same thing about you. Or rather, shouldn't you be?"

His lips quirked into a crooked smile. "Store's closed. Besides, I was wondering if I could take you somewhere.

It's a surprise, so I don't want to give a lot of details away."

"Um, okay." She looked down at her jacket and jeans. "Am I dressed okay?"

"Do you have a beanie for your head? Maybe a scarf to keep you extra warm?"

"I'll be good without them." Plus, she'd never bought the extra winter accessories. She went inside, grabbed her purse then locked the door. "I'm ready."

"Great." His head cocked, motioning for her to follow.

As they walked toward the front of the general store, Vivian broke the silence. "Michael, I just want to say—"

"Please wait." He held up a hand. "Please, just let me show you the surprise, then we can talk."

She bit her lip. "Okay."

"Thank you."

She nodded, then froze. Before her stood a horse-drawn carriage. "What?" she breathed.

"I wanted to take you on a little tour. You interested?"

Was she? Vivian grinned. "Of course. I thought these things only existed in the movies."

"It is Christmas in Willow Springs."

"You should have pointed this little adventure out my first day here." She took the hand he offered and stepped into the carriage. There were blankets and to-go mugs. "What's in there?"

"Hot chocolate."

"Perfect."

Once she had a to-go cup in hand, Michael grabbed the reins and directed the horses.

"Can I ask where we're going?"

"Downtown on Main Street."

That was going to be gorgeous. The whole street had been decorated for the season, and Vivian couldn't wait to see if it looked more festive from the seat of a carriage versus walking on the sidewalk.

"Listen, Vivian."

She looked at Michael.

"I want you to know I respect your need for space. But I also wanted to ensure that you know how repentant I truly am. I promise you, I don't make the same foolish mistakes twice." He gulped. "This surprise is to prove that to you. I also wanted to show you how much the community cares—how much *I* care."

"Michael," she whispered softly. "You didn't have to go to any trouble."

He met her gaze. "Yes, I did."

Silence fell between them as they drew closer to Main Street. The lack of conversation wasn't uncomfortable—more reflective on Vivian's part. She wondered what Michael was thinking and what the surprise entailed.

The horses guided the carriage onto Main Street, and Vivian could barely stop her gasp at the wonder of the evening. People milled about, and the street was illuminated by all the Christmas lights around the storefronts.

"Willow Springs is so beautiful this time of year," she murmured.

"Wait until you see spring."

She could only imagine. She scanned around, taking in everything, then stopped on a couple. "Hey, that's the Diaz family." She blinked in surprise as they waved to her.

"It is. They wanted you to know how much they appreciate your commitment to the Christmas Wishes program." Michael pointed across the street. "And that's Jimmie's parents. They've got one happy kid who enjoys learning now that his class environment fits his at-home needs."

"What have you done?" She stared at him in shock.

"Every person who received their Christmas wish came out tonight. With a few phone calls here and there, I told them my plan. You'll notice them waving." He pointed to another family, who were indeed doing so. They even held a thank-you sign. "The only person who couldn't be here was Stacey. She already took her flight to visit her family."

Vivian teared up. "I can't believe this."

"Not everyone in Willow Springs believes the rumors *or* cares about your past. What they value is your now. How you greet them with a smile at church. How you orchestrated ways to meet every nominee's need. How you are a genuinely kind person. That's what matters to us. That's why we all want you to stay and be a part of this community."

She could barely hold back the tears as his sweet words washed over her. "I'm not leaving. I decided that before you asked me out tonight." She blinked. "I mean, out here. For the surprise. Not that this is a date." She clamped her mouth shut as her cheeks held in volcanic levels of heat.

"I would love for this to be a date," Michael murmured.

"Really?"

He nodded.

Vivian let her grin fly free. "Then it's a date."

Michael grinned back, then they both gasped as snowflakes began falling from the sky.

This was the best Christmas ever.

Michael looked down the row he sat in with Vivian and his siblings in the church sanctuary. His sisters had made it safely back, and Chuck had showed up with a surprising grin. Michael felt the tide turning and prayed that meant good things coming all their ways.

An usher stopped by the end of his row and lit Michael's candle. "Merry Christmas, Big Mike."

"Merry Christmas to you, too." Michael turned and lowered his candle to light Vivian's wick. "You look beautiful in candlelight."

She blushed. "Flattery will get you your Christmas gift."

"Ha. You already gave it to me." The snow globe with the tiny house in it had been placed on his office desk right after he'd opened the gift.

"That was a token." She spoke in low tones. "Your real gift is at my house. I was merely waiting for Christmas Day."

Michael had been surprised to find out this was Vivian's first candlelight service. Then again, her parents hadn't taken her to church growing up. He'd made sure that Vivian knew they were invited to join them for Christmas dinner. They'd eagerly accepted the invitation and would be driving up to join the Wood family for dinner in a few hours.

After everyone had their candles lit, the worship team led them in a rendition of "Joy to the World." Michael's heart filled to bursting as he stared around the church. The sanctuary had been cleaned up, and no traces of graffiti remained. Even better, his ex-tenants had admitted to the vandalism. Apparently, they'd imbibed too much and thought tagging the place would be comical. They'd been charged with the appropriate crimes. As word spread throughout the town, a couple of people had come up to Vivian and personally apologized for feeding into the rumors.

She'd been gracious and accepted their apologies without fanfare. Michael could tell they'd been surprised at her kindness, but that was Vivian. Sweet down to her bones. They'd talked all last night after the carriage ride, and she'd freely shared about her past and the changes her faith had brought.

Her openness had made him more ashamed of how he'd reacted, but she shut down his feelings of guilt, making him promise not to hold on to how he'd reacted. As she said, "Emotions are emotions. What matters is how we move forward."

Like he said, Vivian was sweet down to her bones, and Michael was grateful that she'd forgiven him. He couldn't wait to celebrate Christmas dinner with her by his side and his family in the house.

After a few more songs, the service broke up and candles were extinguished. Soon, Michael found himself back in the kitchen at his house readying the food.

Mr. Dupre watched as Michael carved large cuts of the turkey. "So you fried that, huh?"

"Sure did, sir. It's the best."

"Can't say I've had fried turkey, but it sure does smell good."

Michael smiled at Vivian's father. He'd been nervous to meet her parents, especially knowing she'd probably informed them of his previous missteps. But they'd both been gracious. So he put Vivian's words into practice and let go of his guilt.

"It was kind of your wife to bring those pies."

Mr. Dupre grinned. "I'm a huge fan of my wife's pies. I might have begged. Not to say anything against whatever dessert y'all prepared, but trust me, you're in for a treat."

"I believe you, sir. Anyone who can make a pie look that appetizing has to have skills." Michael still couldn't believe she'd put Christmas stockings on the lattice.

Mr. Dupre carried the turkey to the table as Michael grabbed gravy, stuffing and a couple of other platters. The others had gotten most of the trays onto the dining table. He'd found the table extender in the house earlier so they could be sure to have room for everyone.

As Michael sat at the end of the table, he thought of Pop and his mom and how much joy they'd always brought to the home. *I pray we do the same for generations to come. Love you, Mom and Pop.* Michael bowed his head as Chuck said grace.

"Amen," they chorused.

They passed dishes around, and chatter filled the house. Michael couldn't believe how happy he was to have everyone under the same roof, including Vivian's parents. And knowing that Jordan would be staying after the holidays and not returning to Fayetteville had already eased his stress. Yes, God had blessed them abundantly this Christmas and Michael was glad he had the right attitude to receive the blessings.

Later that evening, Michael held open the general store door so that Vivian could walk through. Her present was tucked under his arm, all wrapped and ready to be revealed. They'd decided to open gifts just the two of them.

Vivian cleared her throat, as they walked toward her tiny home. "There's something I wanted to talk about."

He reached for her hand, squeezing her fingers. "I'm all ears."

"One thing my sponsor told me was to wait until I hit a year before entering into a romantic relationship."

His stomach tensed. "And you're at seven months, right?" He peered down at her small frame.

"Right."

"So what are you thinking?"

Her breath billowed in the air. "What if we take things

slow, like glacier slow. We can go out, here and there, but maybe only stick to handholding. Maybe save a first kiss for my one-year sobriety celebration?" She stopped. "I don't want you to think I'm rejecting you."

He shook his head. "I get it. I hear what you're saying and know how committed you are. I agree to your terms, Ms. Dupre."

Relief flooded her eyes. "Great. Let's exchange gifts." She opened her door.

"Have a seat, and I'll go get your gift," she said, gesturing to the living area.

"Sounds good." He sat down, staring at the square present.

Was the gift good enough for her? He'd tried to figure out a present appropriate for a woman he was just beginning a romantic relationship with but not one that would put pressure on who got whom the best gift. Or maybe he'd just overthought the whole process.

"Got it."

His head whipped up at the sound of her voice. She held a rectangle-shaped box in her hands. "For you."

He took the present and handed her his. "How should we do this? At the same time?"

"No way." She held up her phone. "I'll take a picture of you opening the gift, then you'll do the same for me."

He chuckled. "Yes, ma'am." He ripped the paper right down the middle and reveled in the sound of Vivian's laughter. He shoved the paper away, and his jaw dropped. She'd gotten him a sketch of an elk. "How did you know?"

"I asked Jordan what your favorite things were, and she told me you liked elks. Then when I was downtown last week looking for last-minute gifts—" she smiled sheepishly "—I saw it and just knew."

"I love it. This is great."

She beamed.

"Your turn."

He wanted to laugh, knowing what he'd bought and what she'd gifted him. They'd both had pictures in mind.

Vivian gasped. "How in the world did you manage this?" She held up the photo of them grinning in the horse-drawn carriage.

"Apparently Mrs. Diaz snapped the picture. She thought I might like it. I convinced Maddie to print off a copy at the photography store and sell me a frame to fit. Now you're holding it."

She got up and sat next to him, wrapping an arm around his shoulder. "It's perfection. Thank you so much." She pulled back, and her gaze caught his.

"Was Christmas everything you imagined?" he asked, his voice husky to his own ears.

"It was more."

He slid his hands up her neck to cup her face. "I'm looking forward to many more Christmases with you, Vivian Dupre."

"And I with you, Michael Wood." She placed a kiss on his cheek.

He slipped his arms around her and squeezed her into a hug.

He'd been right, thinking that Vivian Dupre was a danger to his well-ordered life. A life that had needed to be shaken up and turned upside down—not to his detriment, but to change his perspective and align it as God had intended.

He'd be forever grateful that Vivian's redemption had led her to Willow Springs, for she had brightened up his life more than all the downtown Christmas lights ever could.

Epilogue

One year later.

Vivian hung the black ornament on the branch and paused. She tilted her head to see around the tree and into Michael's happy face. "Can you believe it's Christmas time already? It seems like yesterday that this was my first time decorating the tree for the store." She stepped back to grab another ornament, but before she could, Michael took her hand in his.

"Actually I can. Time seems to go by swiftly when I'm with you. Proof you're the reason my days are so bright." He tucked a strand of her behind her ear.

"Aw, babe." She squeezed his hands. "I can't believe the sweet things you say to me sometimes."

His grin grew mischievous. "Are you saying you didn't know the first time you laid eyes on me that I was going to turn out to be Mr. Right?"

She laughed. "I wanted nothing to do with you. And there came Ms. Ann putting us in charge of Christmas Wishes."

"Something I thank God for every night when I pray."

Her eyes teared up and she sniffed. "Again with the sweet words."

"I can't help it, Vivian. It's like I was operating with half a heart before meeting you. I can't tell you how much I've loved getting to know you better this past year. Or how much I love you. There will never be enough words or enough time to express my love for you, Vivian Dupre."

He dropped to one knee.

"Michael..." Her heart thudded as he pulled a ring out of his pocket.

"But if you would do me the honor of becoming my wife and letting me show you just how much you mean to me, then my prayers will be answered."

When she'd gotten her one-year sobriety chip, Michael had been there to cheer her on. He'd taken her on what he called their first "official" date and they'd shared a kiss afterward. And every day since, he had been there to cheer her on, to share his hopes and dreams with her, and to make new memories as a couple. Michael was truly a gift she never expected.

Vivian would be a fool to deny her heart and ignore every lesson God had taught her thus far. He was good and desired to bless His children, no matter their past. And Vivian would accept the gift of Michael wholeheartedly.

"Yes, Michael Wood. I would love to be your wife."

A *whoop* filled the air as he stood, gathering her into his arms. His full lips fell on hers tenderly and she wrapped her arms around his neck, returning the affection. When he broke the kiss, he tucked her under his chin.

"I love you," she whispered, happiness filling every part of her being.

"And I love you."

Vivian wasn't perfect and Michael surely wasn't either, but they were perfect together. There to lift the other when one was down or simply needed a listening ear.

Michael had taught her so much about love and how much capacity her heart had for him. Every day they were together felt like a gift, but more so this time of year. The Lord continued to show her that her past hadn't been the last chapter, but the start of a lifetime. One filled with Christmas blessings the whole year through.

* * * * *

If you enjoyed this story, don't miss Toni Shiloh's next emotional romance, available next year from Love Inspired!

Find more great reads at www.LoveInspired.com.

Dear Reader,

I want to thank all of you for picking up Michael's and Vivian's story. There are so many books to read and so little time, so thank you for the blessing of your time. I hope you enjoy the story of the first of the Wood siblings.

Vivian and Michael had a lot to work through this Christmas season. I pray that the story brought you hope and reminded you of how amazing the birth of Christ is and how knowing Jesus changes us from the inside out.

If you need help with an alcohol addiction, you can find many resources from Alcoholics Anonymous at https://www.aa.org/.

And if you're interested in knowing more about my writing or need links to my social media sites, please visit my website, http://tonishiloh.com.

Blessings,
Toni

COMING NEXT MONTH FROM
Love Inspired

HER UNLIKELY AMISH PROTECTOR
by Jocelyn McClay

Amish nanny Miriam Schrock isn't pleased when handsome bad boy Aaron Raber starts working for the same family as she does. But soon Miriam sees the good man he's become. When his troubled past threatens them both, Aaron must step in to protect the only one who truly believes in him...

THE MYSTERIOUS AMISH NANNY
by Patrice Lewis

Lonely Amish widower Adam Chupp needs help raising his young son. When outsider Ruth Wengerd's car breaks down, she agrees to care for Lucas until it can be repaired. Ruth fits into Amish life easily but is secretive about her past. Will Adam learn the truth about her before he loses his heart?

RESTORING THEIR FAMILY
True North Springs • by Allie Pleiter

Widow Kate Hoyle arrives at Camp True North Springs to heal her grieving family, not the problems of camp chef Seb Costa. But the connection the bold-hearted chef makes with her son—and with her own heart—creates a recipe for love and hope neither one of them expects.

THE BABY PROPOSAL
by Gabrielle Meyer

After his brother's death, Drew Keelan finds himself guardian of his infant nephew. But to keep custody, Drew must get married fast! He proposes a marriage in name only to the baby's aunt, Whitney Emmerson. But when things get complicated, will love help keep their marriage going?

RECLAIMING THE RANCHER'S HEART
by Lisa Carter

Rancher Jack Dolan is surprised when his ex-wife, Kate, returns to town and tells him that they are still married. He suggests that they honor the memory of their late daughter one last time, then go their separate ways. This could be the path to healing—and finding their way back to each other...

THE LONER'S SECRET PAST
by Lorraine Beatty

Eager for a fresh start, single mom Sara Holden comes to Mississippi to help redo her sister's antique shop. And she needs local contractor Luke McBride's help. But the gruff, unfriendly man wants nothing to do with Sara. Can she convince him to come out of seclusion and back to life?

LOOK FOR THESE AND OTHER LOVE INSPIRED BOOKS WHEREVER BOOKS ARE SOLD, INCLUDING MOST BOOKSTORES, SUPERMARKETS, DISCOUNT STORES AND DRUGSTORES.

LICNM1122